Coming Full Circle

A childhood friends to lovers small town romance

Pembrooke series

Jessica Prince

Discover Other Books by Jessica

<u>WHITECAP SERIES</u>
Crossing the Line
My Perfect Enemy

<u>WHISKEY DOLLS SERIES</u>
Bombshell
Knockout
Stunner
Seductress
Temptress
Vamp

<u>HOPE VALLEY SERIES:</u>
Out of My League
Come Back Home Again

The Best of Me
Wrong Side of the Tracks
Stay With Me
Out of the Darkness
The Second Time Around
Waiting for Forever
Love to Hate You
Playing for Keeps
When You Least Expect It
Never for Him

REDEMPTION SERIES

Bad Alibi

Crazy Beautiful

Bittersweet

Guilty Pleasure

Wallflower

Blurred Line

Slow Burn

Favorite Mistake

Sweet Spot

THE CLOVERLEAF SERIES:

Picking up the Pieces
Rising from the Ashes
Pushing the Boundaries

Worth the Wait

<u>THE COLORS NOVELS:</u>
Scattered Colors
Shrinking Violet
Love Hate Relationship
Wildflower

<u>THE LOCKLAINE BOYS (a LOVE HATE RELATIONSHIP spinoff):</u>
Fire & Ice
Opposites Attract
Almost Perfect

<u>THE PEMBROOKE SERIES (a WILDFLOWER spinoff):</u>
Sweet Sunshine
Coming Full Circle
A Broken Soul

<u>CIVIL CORRUPTION SERIES</u>
Corrupt
Defile
Consume
Ravage

<u>GIRL TALK SERIES:</u>

Seducing Lola

Tempting Sophia

Enticing Daphne

Charming Fiona

<u>STANDALONE TITLES:</u>

One Knight Stand

Chance Encounters

Nightmares from Within

<u>DEADLY LOVE SERIES:</u>

Destructive

Addictive

Pembrooke Playlist

"Room to Breathe" by You Me At Six

"Till It's Gone" by Yelawolf

"Talking Body" by Tove Lo

"Riptide" by Vance Joy

"Way Down We Go" by Kaleo

"Landslide" by Fleetwood Mac

"Gods & Monsters" by Lana Del Ray

"Unsteady" by X Ambassador

"Edge of Seventeen" by Stevie Nicks

"I'm Comin' Over" by Chris Young

"Burning Man" by Dierks Bentley and Brothers Osborne

"Girl Like You" by Jason Aldean

"Paint It, Black" by The Rolling Stones

"Ramble On" by Led Zeppelin

Prologue

Eliza

I FELL IN love with Ethan Prewitt when I was nine years old.

It wasn't *real* love or anything. I was only nine —almost ten—after all, but back then it was the most intense, consuming emotion I'd ever experienced in my young life. From nine to twelve I was a blushing, giggling, stuttering mess whenever he was around, and seeing as my Dad and his wife Chloe were best friends with Ethan's sister and brother-in-law, he was around *a lot*.

Ethan was gorgeous and popular and way too old for me — which only added to the thrill of it. But as time passed and we really got to know each other, that young, childish love evolved. I started to grow up, mature, and that immature infatuation turned into a friendship the likes of which I cherished above all else.

My relationship with Ethan was the most important thing in my life. It was him I went to when I needed advice, his opinion I held in the highest regard, his shoulder I leaned on whenever I needed someone to share my burdens with. As the years passed, that respect only grew.

He turned into the best friend I could have ever had. We told each other everything, confiding things we wouldn't dare tell anyone else. We shared our ambitions and dreams. We knew each other better than anyone else. I needed him. I grew to depend on him.

And looking back, I realized that was my biggest mistake.

Because needing someone didn't necessarily mean they needed you back. It was a lesson I'd learned even before Ethan came into my life. You could give a person all the love you were capable of carrying, but that didn't mean you'd get the same in return.

My mother hadn't taught me much in my life, but that particular lesson was the one that stuck the most, sad as it was.

There were people in your life who were supposed to care, supposed to do their best to protect you from all the bad. My father was one of those people, his wife

Chloe another. It hurt to know my own mother, my flesh and blood, wasn't one of those people, and for that very reason, I kept my circle small. Only those who I'd go to the ends of the earth for and who I trusted to do the same for me were allowed in. I appreciated quality over quantity, and while keeping people out sometimes led to being lonely, I'd convinced myself that it was enough. I had everyone I'd ever need. I had Dad and Chloe, Noah and Harlow, my other friend Lilly.

And I had Ethan. Or so I thought.

I only had him for six years before I lost him.

Then I spent the next six regretting the fact that I ever let Ethan Prewitt in.

Chapter One

Ethan

IT WAS YET another sleepless night where I spent hours staring up at the slow spinning ceiling fan above my bed. I tried counting the rotations hoping the monotony would clear my head enough to let drowsiness take over, but no such luck. I hadn't slept for shit since I took that hit on the field. The hit that fucked my knee to hell and took me out of the game for the rest of the season. I'd lived and breathed football for as long as I could remember, and now that it had been taken from me, I was left with nothing to do but think.

Not a good thing, especially since sitting idle was something I'd been avoiding like the plague for the past six years.

The warm, naked body next to me in the bed shifted and ripped me from my thoughts. How sad was it that

I'd been so lost in my own head that I'd forgotten the woman sleeping next to me?

"Mmm," she hummed pleasurably. "Good morning, handsome."

My head rolled on the pillow to face the blonde currently pressing her fake tits against my arm. Amber. One of the few women in my phone who got repeat calls... not that those calls were all that often. But seeing as I was holed up in my apartment with a goddamned torn ACL and unable to hit up the clubs and bars with my teammates to pick up a random hookup for the night, my choices were limited.

Unfortunately, that also meant I'd been left with no choice but to invite her to my place if I wanted to get laid — something I made a conscious effort *never* to do until now.

"Morning," I muttered, sounding sullen despite having marathon sex last night with a woman more than happy to do all the work.

"You don't sound too happy," she purred, running her bright red nails across my chest. "How about I do something to put you in a better mood?"

My hands went to her hips and grabbed hold, stopping her just before she managed to throw her leg over my hip and straddle my waist. "Sorry, babe. PT will be here any minute, so I'm gonna have to take a rain check."

When her bottom lip jutted out in a pout, it took everything I had not to roll my eyes. But since I'd used her for sex and had no intentions whatsoever of calling her again after the night before, I figured the least I could do was be polite to the woman while I attempted to shuffle her out of my apartment.

"Gotta take a leak, then you should probably get going. No need for you to stay and be bored out of your mind while he's working my knee." I shifted her body away from mine and sat up, easing my left leg off the mattress so I could attempt to stand.

I hobbled awkwardly over to my crutches, the long brace on my leg making it more difficult as Amber spoke. "I really don't mind. Maybe I could help you out while you're recovering? Like cleaning and cooking until you can get around a little better?"

Oh Jesus. The hope shining her in eyes — eyes that had mascara streaked underneath, not a very good look — had me twitching to run, and if it wasn't for my blown-out knee, I had no doubt I'd already be locking myself in the bathroom. However, I wasn't that lucky; I was stuck in place while she crawled from the bed, revealing every inch of her body to me as she closed the distance between us.

Her nails traced along the waistband of my boxer briefs as she whispered, "Maybe I'll clean naked. It could be fun." Her lips tilted up in a seductive smile that held little effect since half her makeup had streaked into places it didn't belong, making her look more like a drunk clown than a seductress. My dick didn't so much as twitch.

Fuck me. That was one of the reasons I never had them over to my place, and I never stayed the night at theirs. Things never looked the same in the light of day as they did the night before.

"Maybe some other time, baby." I tried to smile, hoping it didn't look as forced as it felt. "Besides, you wouldn't want to put my cleaning lady Rosita out of work, now would you?" I gave her a little wink and let go of one of my crutches long enough to smack her on the ass.

As I pivoted toward the bathroom, the sound of my front door opening and closing sounded, followed by a loud voice. "Wake your lazy ass up, Prewitt. Time to get this shit started."

That time my grin wasn't fake at all. I probably shouldn't have looked so damned giddy, but I couldn't help it. Typically I hated PT, but just then I could have kissed Duke for saving me from having to physically remove Amber from my apartment.

"Looks like it's time to go, sweetness. I'll give you a call sometime."

With a forlorn expression, she turned and started picking up her clothes, and I took that as my opportunity to take a piss. When I emerged from the bathroom, she was already dressed, but instead of being gone, she was standing next to my bedside table, the picture frame I'd kept there in every single apartment I'd lived in the past six years in her hands.

She looked up with a smile on her face. "Is this you when you were in college? You look so young!"

"Put that down," I grunted as I made my way in her direction. Before she could follow my command, I reached her and snatched the frame from her fingers, placing it back down exactly as it had been. No one touched it but me. Even Rosita knew just to dust around it.

"Sorry," she snapped in a snotty tone as I scooted the picture a centimeter over, tilting it so it could be seen perfectly from my side of the bed. "Is that your sister or cousin or something?"

I looked back down at the photo in question, taking in Eliza's bright, shining smile. My sister Harlow had taken it. She had a gift for photography and snapped the picture just as Eliza's head was tipped back in laughter at something I'd just said to her. My arm was thrown over her shoulder and I was grinning down at her with a pleased-as-shit look on my face that I'd been able to make her laugh. We'd been in my old backyard, it was the same house Harlow and her husband Noah still lived in. It was their daughter Lucy's fifth birthday party, and I'd driven back from college in Laramie to celebrate. It was the first time I'd seen Eliza in weeks. Having a full class load and football practice all the damn time, it had been hard for us to catch up. But when I got home that weekend, we'd picked up right where we left off.

It might have been weird to some, a twenty-one year guy so excited to see a fifteen year old girl, but it wasn't like that. She was my best friend. The best friend I'd *ever* had. I never felt the age gap when we were together. Maybe it was because she'd already experienced shit at a young age that no kid should have to go through, but she was mature... and so damn smart. And because of the shit her mom had put her through, she could understand feeling like an outsider. That was probably what bonded us the most.

Then I'd fucked it all up. Because about a year after that picture was taken, my feelings started to change. Feelings that fucked with my head in a major way and scared the hell out of me. Feelings I'd convinced myself were all kinds of wrong. Feelings I never, *ever* planned to act on.

So I left. I had no choice.

And the worst thing about it was, in the six years I'd been gone, my feelings hadn't lessened in the slightest.

"She's my best friend," I answered.

"Isn't she a little..." Amber's words trailed off, drawing my gaze away from the picture and back to her, "*young* to be your best friend?"

"We practically grew up together," I ground out, feeling an overwhelming sense of protectiveness where my relationship with Eliza Anderson was concerned, even if it wasn't the complete truth. It was the same feeling I felt for years any time someone questioned our friendship, or said anything negative about her in general. Because of my stupidity, we hadn't spoken in six years, but to this day, that desire to defend her, to defend what we had, hadn't lessened in the slightest.

Even if I didn't have her anymore.

"I need to get a quick shower," I grumbled as I used my crutches to help me pivot around, giving Amber my back. "I'm sure you can see your way out."

"So..." she called out hesitantly, but I didn't stop moving. "You'll call me?"

Not a fucking chance in Hell. "Sure. I'll be pretty busy with rehab and stuff, but I'll give you a call if I have time." With that, I shut the bathroom door on her. I trusted Duke to keep her from stealing any of my shit, and after the hard hit that thinking about Eliza caused, I was done.

As I stood under the hot shower spray, I went over the hundred ways I spent the past six years being the world's biggest asshole. It started with hurting the one person I was the closest with and ended with me waiting so long to apologize and make things right, that it was already too late. Looking back, I could have done things differently. But you know what they say about hindsight.

It's a motherfucker.

MY CELLPHONE RANG JUST AS I POPPED A COUPLE ibuprofen and downed then with the cold beer in my hand. Duke had left an hour ago, but because he was a sadist, my knee was throbbing like hell, which did nothing to help improve my earlier mood.

I reached into the pocket of my sweats and pulled the phone out, not bothering to look at the display as I answered with a curt, "What?"

"Holy shit!" a familiar voice cried from the other end. "He actually answered the phone! Noah! Quick! Look out the window and tell me if the world's on fire. This has to be the sign of the apocalypse."

"You're fucking hysterical, Low-Low," I dead-panned. "To what do I owe the pleasure?"

"What? Can't a sister call her baby brother and give him shit for being an asshole who never comes to see her or her family and barely has the time to talk on the phone anymore?"

My head dropped down as I rested a hand on the dark granite of the kitchen island and leaned forward. With a sigh, I told her, "I'm really not in the mood for this right now, Harlow."

"I don't give two shits what you're in the mood for Ethan. Last I heard from you, you were about to have surgery to repair the tear to your ACL. That was *eight days ago*! I had to hear from your *agent* that you were doing well and at home recuperating. You haven't answered a single call, you won't return any of my messages, and Noah said you've been ignoring him too. What the hell, man?"

"Harlow—"

Doing what she always did and ignoring the warning in my tone, she pushed forward. "Lucy's been worried about you, and Evan's been beside himself since he saw you take that hit. Do you have any idea how hard it is to try and console a six-year-old when he thinks his favorite uncle just got his guts stomped on the field?"

"I'm his only uncle," I replied, but she wasn't finished.

"I'll tell you. It's really *freaking* hard, Ethan. You're his idol for Christ's sake. Lucy and Evan *adore* you. But you can't even bother with more than one or two goddamned phone calls to let us know you're okay and still alive?!"

By the end of her rant Harlow's voice got so high pitched, I started to worry for the dogs in their neighborhood. But she made her point.

"I'm sorry," I muttered through the line.

"Sorry, what was that? Couldn't hear you since you were mumbling. Try repeating it, and this time try and talk like a grownup."

Just like Harlow to give me shit, even when I was trying to apologize. She had never been one to just accept an apology. Oh no, she made you bust your ass to earn her forgiveness. No one knew that better than me and her husband Noah. She'd practically made the man jump through flaming hoops to win her back after breaking her heart when they were teenagers.

"I said, '*I'm sorry*,'" I repeated, making sure to enunciate. "You're right. I've been a prick."

She was quiet for a few seconds before stating, "Yes. You have."

"I'm really sorry, Low-Low," I said softly, using the

nickname I'd given her when I was little, hoping it would help to butter her up. "I'll make it up to you guys. I promise."

"Good. Because I've already told the kids Uncle Ethan's coming for an extended visit starting next week."

"You *what*?!"

"And don't worry. I've already cleared it with your agent and, lucky you, Fletch is a licensed physical therapist! What a coincidence, huh?"

It was bullshit was what it was. I wouldn't have been surprised if Harlow had this whole thing planned out, *including* having Noah's assistant coach Fletcher getting certified as a PT. "You're kidding, right? I can't just pick up and leave. I've got shit to do here, Harlow."

"Like what? You're out for the rest of the season and on limited activity until your knee's healed up, so don't give me that. It's been way too long since you've been back home—"

"That's not my home anymore, that's *your* home. Denver's my home."

"Call it whatever you want, but pack your shit. Duke said you can't fly just yet, so Noah and I are driving up to get you next Saturday. We'll crash at your place for the night and head back early Sunday morning."

"You talked to *Duke* too?" I asked incredulously.

"What can I say? Everyone around you, *except you,*

thinks your family is freaking awesome. Now pack. I'm done playing this game with you. It's time I had my little brother back."

She hung up before I could say anything.

"Shit," I breathed as I dropped my phone on the counter, suddenly feeling more exhausted than I had before the phone call.

There was no way I was going to be able to talk myself out of this one. I was going back to Pembrooke.

Whether I liked it or not.

Chapter Two

Eliza

"ONE CHICKEN PICCATA in the window," I called out as I set the plate down and moved back to my station to chop more parsley. My body moved as if it were on auto pilot. I didn't even have to think about what to do next. Instinct kicked in and I moved from station to station doing what I loved.

Chop. Dredge. Baste. Mix.

Over and over again.

Cooking was my dream. I loved everything about being in a professional kitchen — the smells, the sounds, the praise from customers when they appreciated something I'd made for them.

I'd been telling my father I was going to be a professional chef ever since my stepmom Chloe took me into her kitchen and taught me how to bake my first cupcake. And there I was, more than ten years later living my dream.

When I graduated from Wyoming's Culinary Institute two years ago, I hadn't really had a plan for where I wanted to go. I just knew I needed to be in the kitchen. As a graduation present, Dad and Chloe had taken me to Sinful Sweets, the bakery Chloe had opened when I was a little girl. I'd always loved that place. In all my years, I had yet to find anyone who baked as well as her. But I didn't just hold an appreciation for pastry. I wanted to cook *everything*. So, imagine my surprise, when they informed me that they were building out the bakery. Where there'd only been room for a few tables and chairs before, the plans now called for a full dining area. The kitchen would also be expanded in order to add room for the new stations where we'd prep and cook meals for lunch and dinner.

Sinful Sweets Bakery had turned into Sinful Sweets Café. Chloe would still handle the baking side of the business, but they had given me my very own kitchen. Instead of being a place where you could stop in and get coffee and sweets, we now served a full meal for lunch and dinner. And the best part was, the menu was *all mine*. I could cook whatever I was in the mood to cook.

And I did.

Sure, it wasn't a five-star restaurant or anything like that, and we'd never win a Michelin star, but I was happy. I had the career I loved, in the town I loved, surrounded by my closest friends and family.

In order to keep things from getting stale and boring, the menu changed daily. The specials were always different, so the people of Pembrooke got a new surprise every time they walked in. Today's lunch special was chicken piccata. And just like every day since we re-opened two years ago, it was a hit.

"God, I don't think I'll ever get used to how amazing it smells in here."

I spun around to find Chloe standing just inside the door that led out into the alley behind the building. Wiping my hands on a clean dishtowel, I looked over at Gary, one of my line cooks and asked him to take over for me.

"What are you doing here?" I grinned as I walked over to give her a tight hug. "Aren't you supposed to be on vacation? Dad's going to have a conniption if he finds out you came into work when you were supposed to be relaxing."

She waved me off. "He'll get over it. I'm at home bored out of my mind, and it's all his fault."

"How dare he try and force you into taking some

time off for the first time in three years? What an asshole!" I said on a laugh.

"Language," she admonished with a scowl.

I shot her a wink and told her the same thing I'd been saying for the past few years. "Adult now, Chlo." I pointed at my chest. "I have a 401K, my own medical and dental, and I no longer live under your and Dad's roof. Hate to break it to you, but with that comes the privilege of cussing."

"Don't remind me," she muttered sullenly. "I still remember when you were little and were perfectly content with following me around the kitchen all day long. I miss that."

"I'm still in the kitchen with you most days."

She actually pouted as she said, "Yeah, but it's not the same. Now you're running your own section. You're all grown up. I don't know if I like it."

"Hey, you still have Catelyn and Abigale. At least you've got several more years to boss them around."

She crossed her arms over her chest and rolled her eyes. "Please. Like you aren't totally aware your heathen sisters are little spawns of your father. Did he tell you we caught Cate giving Abbi a haircut two days ago?"

"No," I gasped, wide-eyed that my seven-year old little sister had actually taken a pair of scissors to five-year old Abbi's head. "How bad?"

"*Bad.* And it didn't help that she tried to glue it back on herself when she discovered her older sister was a terrible hair dresser."

I couldn't help but crack up at the visual she'd just painted for me. Truth was, I could totally see my little sisters doing something like this. For someone who exuded an air of badassery on a daily basis, my father was a total pushover when it came to his girls, myself included. The people of Pembrooke would be shocked to see just how whipped Sheriff Anderson, the man they'd elected into position, was for all of the Anderson girls. But maybe that's what made him so good at his job. He came home to an estrogen fest every evening. He had to get his aggression out somewhere, right?

Anyway, Abbi and Cate's desire to follow Dad around like I used to follow Chloe, combined with his inability to tell them no, helped to breed two girls with tomboy tendencies, very little fear, and *way* too much curiosity. Chloe was right. They were *just like* my father. To say their house was chaotic on a good day was putting it mildly. But I knew she secretly loved it.

"So, what?" I asked once I was able to speak through my laughter. "You came to escape for a few hours?"

Suddenly all the earlier humor fled from her expression and she grew uncharacteristically serious. "Think you can take a break for a few minutes? In private?"

"Uh, sure. Let's go upstairs." My stomach twisted into knots as I turned to tell Gary he was in charge for the time being and took off my cook jacket before heading out to the stairs.

Chloe's old apartment over the bakery had also undergone renovations when the café expanded. It now not only ran the length of the bakery and restaurant, but also over the top of the dance studio that my childhood friend Lilly ran next door. Seeing as we worked right next to each other and had been best friends for years, we'd turned the place from a studio into a two bedroom/two bathroom apartment so we could be room-mates. It cut costs for both of us, and came with the added benefit of getting us out from under our parents' roofs. It was a win-win.

We were sitting on the large, overstuffed couch in the living room, and it took several seconds before I finally got the nerve to ask, "What's up? You're kind of freaking me out right now. Is everything okay with Dad and the girls?"

"No, no. Everyone's fine. It's nothing like that, I just... I wanted to tell you before you found out through the Pembrooke grapevine. Gossip around here's already bad enough as it is. Hell, I'm surprised you haven't already heard—"

The tension in my chest loosened but anxiety still

coursed through my system. "Heard what?" I cut in. "Jeez, Chloe. Just tell me already, you're starting to worry me."

She sucked in a big breath and looked me straight in the eye. "Ethan's coming back."

It was as though my brain couldn't compute what she'd just said. "Ethan's coming back," I repeated flatly. "Back where? Back *here?*"

Chloe swallowed audibly and nodded, suddenly looking very worried. She and Lilly were the only two people who knew just how much Ethan's abandonment had crushed me. They'd both been there, front and center, when I was a little girl who was convinced I was going to marry him one day. And they'd been there when the naivety of those little girl dreams wore off, and what I had with Ethan developed into one of the most important friendships I'd ever had. They were the only two people I had been able to lower my mask in front of. They took my heartbreak over his dismissal of me just as hard as I did, feeling the pain I had been carrying with me over the past six years just as acutely.

And they understood exactly *why* it hurt so badly.

Being raised by a mother who made it clear on a regular basis that she'd wished she never had me made a lasting impression. The only reprieve I'd gotten was when I was with my Dad. When he started seeing

Chloe, she went off the rails, started drinking and disappearing all the time. And when she *was* there, she was even worse than her usually terrible self, constantly needling me for information about Chloe. When I refused to say anything negative, she'd try her best to guilt trip me for preferring some "whore over her own mother." She'd eventually gone so far over the edge that there was no going back, earning herself a few months' jail time, several hefty fines, years of parole, and being stripped of all custody over me until I was old enough to make the decision whether or not I wanted her in my life.

At thirteen, I made the mistake of reaching out even though Dad was against it, thinking that maybe she'd have gotten the wakeup call she needed to actually *be* a mother.

The conversation with her that took place left me flayed open. I experienced a whole new pain I hadn't even realized existed. Dad had been more furious than I'd ever seen him, raging, telling me there was no way in hell I was ever speaking to her ever again. Chloe was disgusted by my mother's behavior and did everything she could to try and make me feel better. But me... well, I was broken. After that, I kept my loved ones close and everyone else closed out. It was still something I struggled with to this very day, opening myself up to trust other people, risking getting hurt again.

When Ethan disappeared from my life, I felt that pain all over again, only that time it was much more acute. You see, I knew what my mother was, always had. In the back of my mind, there was always the knowledge of what she was capable of. But Ethan was different. I looked at him like he'd hung the moon, could do no wrong. I'd been blindsided and in complete disbelief. When I finally managed to get ahold of him, just long enough to demand answers for his abrupt disappearance from my life, all I'd gotten were hateful words that broke my heart into pieces.

The best thing that could have happened after that was him never coming back.

He left me shattered, and I hated him for it.

"Harlow put her foot down. She misses her brother, and her and Noah's kids miss their uncle. I know he hurt you, but Ethan's still their family, sweetheart." The sorrow in her clear green eyes hit me like a gut punch. "I know you heard that he was hurt..."

"Of course I heard," I replied bitterly. "He's like a goddamned legend in this town. It's all anyone was able to talk about for weeks." Despite my hatred for him, Pembrooke adored their golden boy. The kid who was a football prodigy. The one who made it to the NFL. All I wanted was to have him out of my life completely, only to have him shoved down my throat at every turn.

"Well, she got sick of him avoiding his family. Said it's been going on too long, so she and Noah are going to get him. Harlow set it up so he can do the rest of his rehab here."

"So he'll be here for a while?"

"I don't know," she shrugged, "I would assume so. I mean, I know he's out for the rest of the season, and I'd imagine physical therapy and training will take a while to get him back into playing shape." Leaning forward, she placed her hand on mine and squeezed. "I'm sorry, sweetheart. I know how much he hurt you, and I hate that you may have to see him again. I wish there was something I could do to make it all better for you."

That right there was just one of the reasons why I loved Chloe with all my heart. She made it so damned easy. She gave her love so willingly that it was impossible not to return it. But I wasn't the same little girl I'd been before.

Yes, I was broken. My armor was dented and bent, but I was tougher now. And Ethan Prewitt no longer had the power to hurt me. Feigning a casualness I definitely wasn't feeling, I stood from the couch and took a forti-fying breath.

"It's okay," I told her softly. "You don't need to worry about me."

She stood as well, skepticism written on her face. "You sure, honey?"

I shrugged and offered up a smile. "As long as he stays the fuck away from me for as long as he's here, how could there be any problems?"

Chapter Three

Ethan

BEING BACK IN the house I grew up in for the first time in six years was surreal, to say the least. It wasn't as if I'd intentionally planned to avoid Pembrooke and everyone in it when I first left, but the longer I stayed gone, the more excuses I made for keeping my distance, the easier it got. Then it was no longer easy. By the time I wanted to go back to those people, one in particular, it was too late. I'd stayed away for too long.

Jesus, I'd really made a mess of shit.

"Since you can't take the stairs with your crutches very well, we're putting you on the sleeper sofa," Harlow talked as she lugged my bags into the den. "We just got a new mattress for you so it should be comfortable."

"That's fine," I mumbled as I crutched along after

her, Noah following slowly on my heels. I scanned the once familiar room and noticed all the subtle changes that had been made, a new paint color, a wainscoting along the walls, little things like that. "You've remodeled," I said, stating the obvious. "It looks nice."

"Well," my sister huffed as she dropped my luggage on the floor unceremoniously and rested her hands on her hips. "You'd have known if you'd have bothered to come home once or twice in the past six years. A lot of changes have been taking place while you were off being a big shot NFL dickhead who was too busy for his friends and family."

"Harlow," Noah spoke up, warning in his tone.

She threw her arms out at her sides. "What? I'm only saying exactly what everyone else is thinking."

"And you've been at this shit all last night and the entire way home. I think he gets it, Wildflower. You're pissed. Time to stop beating the hell out of a dead horse, yeah?"

When I got Harlow's phone call the other day, I hadn't thought I could possibly feel any worse. I'd been wrong. Knowing I'd hurt my sister with my absence, hurt my whole family, cut like a goddamned knife. When our grandmother had died when I was fourteen, Harlow had uprooted her entire life, leaving behind her job, her friends, to come take care of me. She hadn't even blinked.

"I'm not beating a dead horse," she continued, the two of them arguing like I wasn't standing right there. "I'm just stating facts. One of those facts being that the only time I've managed to see my little brother since he was drafted was when I packed my family up and hauled my happy little ass to Denver. And here's another fact for you!" She really was on a roll. "Sitting in a car for seven hours with one hormonal teenage girl and a little boy with the attention span of a flea is a *nightmare*. But do you hear me complaining about it?"

"Yes," Noah and I said at the same time.

She ignored us both and continued. "*No.* You know why? Because I'd suffer through that nightmare if it meant seeing my baby brother, if it meant those two terrors got to see the uncle they adored. But does he show me the same courtesy?" She let out a humorless laugh. "Oh no! Why should he have to bother himself with something as mindless as considering *other* people, when he knows his sister will do it for him?"

"You're right, babe," Noah said in a placating, yet slightly sarcastic, tone. "You should be nominated for sainthood."

"Damn right I should!" she finished, finally winding

down from the millionth rant I'd had to experience since they showed up at my place the night before.

Knowing just how to calm her down, Noah moved toward his wife and wrapped her in his arms, leaning in to kiss the side of her head. "Time to wind down, baby. Why don't you go upstairs and run yourself a bubble bath, and I'll bring you up a nice, big glass of wine in just a bit. How's that sound?"

Harlow sighed, leaning further into him, and I was hit with that all too familiar pang deep in my chest. The one that made me feel like an interloper, the third wheel in my own home for years. It wasn't that I disapproved of Harlow and Noah's relationship, I truly was happy for them. But I'd spent most of my childhood feeling like I didn't belong anywhere. My parents died when I was so little that I barely remembered what they looked like, and we were sent to live with our grandmother.

Things had been good for a few years, until the day Harlow took off for reasons that were her own. And I'd felt abandoned for the second time in my life. That feeling only got worse when Gram died. Sure, Harlow had given up everything and come back to be with me, but it was only a short time before her and Noah got together. Then she was pregnant and they were starting their own family.

I spent years struggling with where I fit into

everyone else's lives. The weight of feeling like a guest in my own home pressed down on my chest, growing heavier and heavier with each passing year until the desire to escape and build a life of my own, a life where I didn't constantly fear abandonment, became all I could think about. The only time I ever felt a reprieve from that pressure was when I was with Eliza. She was gifted at making me forget I was unhappy. I was happy when I was with her. I could confess everything I was feeling to her without risk of judgment, and she would just make everything... *better*.

And it was for those reasons that I ran.

Because I knew, I *knew* that she was the only person with the power to make me stay. She was the one thing I'd give up my dreams for, and that fucking terrified me. She was my best friend, the one person I depended on above everyone, and I found myself considering giving it all up just to stay close to her. Before I knew it was happening, I'd begun contemplating all the *what ifs*.

What if I didn't enter the draft?

What if I gave up football?

What if I stayed in Pembrooke with her instead of taking off to start *my own* life?

What if, what if, what if.

So I ran. And I never looked back.

The sound of Harlow's voice pulled me from my

musings. "I can't. I need to go pick Evan up from Chloe's before he drives her to drink. Between him and her girls, I wouldn't be surprised if she was already halfway into her second bottle.

I wanted to ask so badly what she was talking about, but after years of consciously avoiding any topic that could have potentially led to the mention of Eliza, Noah and Harlow had eventually stopped mentioning the Andersons altogether. I knew they had two girls and that Derrick Anderson had been elected into the position of Sherriff, but that was about the gist of it.

And I knew that if I gave into that desire and asked, Harlow wouldn't have bothered to tell me anyway. She'd have withheld information as punishment just for the fun of it. I loved my sister, but she could be a little sadistic at times, especially if you'd done something to piss her off. And to say she was mad at me would have been putting it mildly.

Harlow left a few minutes later. Lucy was in her room, avoiding me, and Noah was tucked away in his office going over the playbook and practice schedule for the following week, leaving me alone in a house that was too quiet, with nothing to do but think about what a shitty brother, uncle, and friend I'd turned out to be.

I eventually grew restless. My own company strongly lacking, and boredom having set in, I needed to get the hell out of there. The door to Noah's office was partially open, so I chanced a knock before pushing it the rest of the way.

"Hey man, what's up?" he asked, lifting his head from the thick binder on his desk.

"Nothing. I was just wondering if I could borrow your car for a bit. I'm going a little stir crazy and thought it might be a good idea to get out for a bit."

He looked at me skeptically for several seconds before finally asking, "You sure you're good to drive?"

"Doc cleared me just before we left Denver," I assured him. "I'm good to go as long as it's not a long distance or manual transmission. And seeing as how Harlow'd track my ass down and drag me back if I made a break for it, I think it's safe to say I don't plan on driving very far."

I tried to keep my tone casual, but I knew he picked up the underlying tension when he sat back in the chair and released a heavy sigh. "Look, I know she's been riding your ass pretty hard, but it's just because she's missed you. Just give her a bit. She'll get over it and be back to her usual crazy self in a matter of days."

I braced myself on my crutches and reached up to rub at the back of my neck with one hand. "I get it. Really. Bailing and never coming back was a dick move, but I had my reasons—"

"And that's the same bullshit excuse you've been using whenever we've brought it up to you for the past six years."

"Well, bullshit or not, that's the truth of it. They might not be the best reasons, but they're mine, okay. I'm not saying I went about it the right way. I know I didn't, and I'm sorry for what I put you guys through. But I just needed..." I let out a breath as I struggled to find the right words. "I just needed to get away. I never expected it to be for so long."

I could tell from his expression that he wanted to pry. Years of living under the same roof had taught me that my brother-in-law was a fixer. He wanted to dig into my issues until he came up with a solution. Unfortunately for him, I wasn't in much of a sharing mood. How did you admit to a person who'd busted his ass to give you everything that, irrational as it might be, *he* was just one of many issues I had that pushed me to leave?

I never claimed it was a sane line of thought, but there it was. I was resentful of what Noah and my sister had with each other. They had love, a family of their own, a place to *belong*. It was everything I'd ever wanted, but kept coming up short of achieving. I loved them both to death, but I resented that they had each other when every time I started to feel secure something happened to take that feeling away from me.

Before he could question the motives that had kept me away for so long I spoke. "So you gonna let me borrow your ride, or do you want to play chauffer to me the entire time I'm here?" I gave him the carefree grin I'd perfected over the years, the grin that screamed life was good and there were no problems in the world. That grin was a lie, but he didn't need to know that. "I'm all for the whole *Driving Miss Daisy* thing. I can even sit in the back seat to help you get into character."

With a roll of his eyes, he shifted in his seat, reaching into his pocket to retrieve his keys. "Try not to wreck it," he said, tossing them to me. "Your sister'll have my ass if you get hurt again, and with you here, I'm no longer the one in the hot seat. I'd like to keep that streak going as long as possible."

My smile became more genuine the moment the cool metal of the keys touched my palm. "I'll do my best."

As I shifted my crutches and started for the door, he called out from behind me. "Curfew's midnight, shit-head."

I kept going as his laughter followed me down the hallway. I couldn't wait to get rid of those fucking crutches so I had a free hand to flip him off next time he made a smartass comment like that.

I DROVE AIMLESSLY, FOLLOWING THE DIRT PATHS made by years of tires through the mountains I'd grown up in. I let my mind clear of everything as I soaked up the landscape surrounding me. Being in nature like this was the type of solitude I didn't mind. With so much beauty all around me, it was difficult to concentrate on the downward spiral my life seemed to have taken.

By the time I made it down the mountain and back into town, the sun had set. The streetlamps all through the downtown area lit up, giving Pembrooke a quaint glow as I slowed the truck to a crawl and took in the changes to the town I'd grown up in. There weren't many really — the auto body shop on the corner of Main and Sycamore had been replaced with one of those chain pharmacies, there was now a Starbucks on the outskirts of town, and Hal's Hardware had become Hal & Son's Hardware. But despite the fact that everything appeared to be the same, it felt different. I'd grown up here, so much of this place used to be engrained in me, yet as I made my way down the roads with the wooden boardwalk sidewalks, I felt like little more than a tourist.

And something about that realization sat like lead in my stomach. I couldn't remember wanting anything more than to escape this place, but now that I was back, taking it all in, there was a sadness creeping in that it was no longer a part of me.

It wasn't until I pulled in front of one storefront in particular that I put Noah's truck into park and cut the ignition in order to fully absorb what I was seeing.

What used to be Sinful Sweets Bakery was now Sinful Sweets Café. And it was… bigger. Much bigger. From the looks of it, they'd added a restaurant that more than doubled the size of the original bakery. The lights inside were turning off, like it was closing down for the night, and as I watched from across the street I couldn't help but wonder when Chloe had decided to expand.

Then the glass front door of the café opened, and I completely forgot what had caught my attention just moments before. Because I recognized who'd just stepped through and was now locking the place up. Everything inside of me froze solid at the sight of her. The last time I saw her she'd been a girl growing into a woman, but the beauty I was suddenly staring at was *all* woman. All hints of the girl were completely gone, and that pang at the sight of her hit my chest again. The loss so acute it almost stole my breath.

Christ, she'd grown up. I didn't know why that thought surprised me so much, but it did. I guess I always imagined her looking exactly like she had the last time I saw her. I'd never stopped to consider what she would look like as an adult, but what I saw just then left me completely stunned.

Not having seen me, she turned and began down the boardwalk in the opposite direction, and something inside of me revolted at the thought of letting her get away. It was as though my body had a mind of its own, not bothering to communicate with my brain as my hand opened the door to the truck. Before I knew it, I had a ball cap pulled low over my eyes and my crutches beneath my arms. I was limping after her at a slow pace, making sure not to draw her attention. I wasn't sure what I wanted to achieve with my little stalking expedition.

All I knew was that I wasn't ready to let Eliza out of my sight just yet. Now that I'd actually laid eyes on her something told me it would be impossible to stay away.

Chapter Four

Eliza

P*ast*

DAD WAS STILL RAGING. I COULD HEAR HIM shouting and cussing from his and Chloe's bedroom before I had enough of his anger and her sad, watery eyes and took off to the back deck. I knew they were both upset *for* me, but that didn't mean I wanted to deal with it just then.

"Thought you might be out here, kiddo."

The unexpected sound of Ethan's voice startled me. I had just enough time to reach up and dash the tears off my cheeks as he rounded the side of the house before coming and taking a seat next to me on the deck stairs.

Too embarrassed to face him now that he knew I was sitting outside crying, I kept my head bent and let my hair act as a curtain between us. Ethan and I were actually starting to become pretty good friends lately, but that didn't mean I wanted him to see me crying like a baby out here all by myself. "What are you doing here?"

"Chloe called Harlow."

"Of course she did," I replied angrily, wiping at my still wet face since the tears refused to stop. "I'm fine, you know. I don't need you to sit out here and babysit me like I'm some dumb kid."

I knew I was being rude to him for no good reason, he wasn't the one who'd hurt me after all, but I couldn't help it. Even knowing it wasn't his fault, I wanted to lash out in the hopes of making someone else feel just as badly as I did.

"Hey," he said in a soft voice, leaning close so he could bump my shoulder with his. "Look at me for a sec."

I didn't want to. I didn't want him to see my face all red and splotchy from crying. Even though we were becoming friends, I still had a little bit of a crush on him. I knew nothing could ever happen, he was nineteen and I was only thirteen, but he was still the cutest guy I'd ever seen. And right at that moment I looked like a gross mess. When I refused to meet his eyes, he used his fingers to gently lift my face to his. His beautifully strange yellowish-green eyes smiled down at me, and just like always, I thought they had to have been the prettiest eyes I'd ever seen before on a boy or a girl. Depending on what color he was wearing, sometimes they actually looked gold.

"There she is," he grinned at me, "still as pretty as always."

Despite the fluttering in my belly, I still rolled my eyes, because I knew there was no way I looked pretty just then. I was a very ugly crier. My nose got red and swollen and it looked like hives had broken out around my eyes. There was no doubt in my mind that he was just trying to cheer me up.

"Liar," I sniffled, wiping at my face with the back of my hand. "I probably look horrible right now."

"Nah. Not possible."

The flutters in my stomach got stronger as we fell into silence, gazing out at the trees that surrounded my dad's house. I normally loved to stare out into the forest, but at that moment, I wasn't seeing much of what was in front of me. I was too sad.

"You want to talk about it?" Ethan asked a few minutes later. "You don't have to if you don't want."

I swallowed past the lump that had formed in my throat all of a sudden. "I called my mom today," I whispered in a tear-filled, scratchy voice. "Dad didn't want me to at first, but Chloe talked him into letting me. I figured that since it's been three years she might have missed me or something." I squeezed my eyes closed and bowed my head, sucking in a stuttered breath. "It was stupid."

He bumped me again, only this time he didn't pull away from me. "Wanting to talk to your mom isn't stupid, Eliza."

I sniffled again, quickly losing the fight on keeping my emotions at bay. "S-she said..." My voice broke on a hiccough, and I began sobbing uncontrollably. "She said she doesn't want anything to do with me. That if she'd never had me, then her life wouldn't have turned out so messed up, and that she wishes she'd just had an abortion like my Aunt Lilith told her to do. She said I was the worst thing that ever happened to her, and she never wants to see me for as long as she lives."

Each word spoken was like a stab directly to my chest. Reliving those hateful words my own mother had spit at me through the phone was just as painful as the first time I'd heard them. By the time she'd hung up on me, I was an inconsolable mess. When I was finally able to get the words out, Dad was so angry he punched a hole right through the wall and cut his hand up.

Ethan's whole body went stiff beside me after I finished telling him what she'd said. He remained that way for so long I started to worry. Finally, he turned to look at me and the fury in his eyes looked an awful lot like I'd seen in my father's earlier. "No offense, babe, but your mom's a total bitch."

A surprised laugh bubbled up from my throat. "Yeah. She really is."

"And she's totally wrong." My gaze jerked up to his at the unexpected harshness in his voice. "She's so wrong. You're the best thing that ever happened to her, and if she's too fucking stupid to realize that, then it's her loss. I hope she spends the rest of her miserable life bitter and alone."

"Uh..." I breathed, unsure what to say. I figured he'd have been upset on my behalf when I told him what went down, especially considering we were friends, but I hadn't expected his reaction would be so strong. "Thanks, I guess?"

At my response, some of the hardness in his face softened and he smiled at me. "You're sweet and funny, and a great person to be around. She should have felt blessed to have someone as great as you in her life."

His praise, while heartwarming left me feeling a

little awkward. "You have to say that because our families are, like, best friends. You're just being nice."

"When have you known me to say something I didn't mean just to be nice?"

That question gave me pause, because in all the time I'd known Ethan Prewitt, I'd never known him to say anything he didn't mean.

At my lack of response, he smirked. "See? I'm not saying it just to be nice. I'm saying it because it's a fact. And I know it's a fact because you're one of the best friends I've ever had. I know your bitch of a mom should feel lucky because *I* feel lucky that I get to know you."

My jaw dropped opened as I stared into his earnest expression. "Really?"

With a chuckle, he threw his arm over my shoulder and pulled me against him. "Really, kiddo."

It was that day, that very moment that solidified Ethan's place as my best friend.

And that friendship only grew stronger from there.

Chapter Five

Eliza

MY PHONE CHIRPED from my back pocket. Pulling it out, I smiled at the text I just received.

Lilly: *EMERGENCY! We're out of wine!*

I chuckled under my breath as I typed my response.

Eliza: *Then you should have taken your lazy ass to the store. You're right upstairs!*

Lilly: *But my bestest friend is just now getting off work, and I've already taken my bra off for the evening. Don't make me put it back on! Pretty pleeeeeeease?*

I rolled my eyes and gave in, just like I always did.

Eliza: *Fine, since I'm such a nice person I'll run to the corner store. But you owe me.*

Lilly: *Ooh! Pick up those new mega-stuffed Oreo's*

while you're there! And those Oreo churros! Oh! And some chips and salsa!

It was obvious someone was suffering from a major case of PMS. I didn't bother responding back, because honestly, everything she'd just listed off sounded pretty damn good to me. And the bonus was I didn't have to cook any of it.

Flipping the switch to the remaining lights, I walked out the front of Sinful Sweets Café and locked up behind me. Usually, I'd have just taken the back staircase up to my and Lilly's apartment, but since I was her errand bitch for the evening, I hit the boardwalk along Main to stroll the few blocks to Mabel's Corner Market.

The sun was down and the streets were emptying out for the evening. Only a few people were left on the wooden sidewalks. I got a couple friendly "hellos" and chin tilts from the few familiar faces still out and about as I pulled the door open and stepped out of the brisk fall air into the small, quaint store.

"Evening, Eliza."

My head turned toward the front counter where Mabel stood, just like she did every day for as long as I could remember. Well into her seventies, Mabel herself was probably just as much an institution in Pembrooke as her Corner Market was.

"Evening Mabel." I smiled, reaching over to pick up one of the small shopping baskets. "How are you doing?"

"Woke up this morning, so you won't hear me complaining."

"Way to stay positive, Mabel," I laughed as I started for the freezer section. I grabbed the churros from the dessert aisle then bee-lined for the cookies. I heard the bell over the door chime just as I was internally debating the perfect chip/dip combo, when the tiny hairs on my arm suddenly stood on end.

I stood frozen in place as I was hit with a scent I knew all too well. It was like clean cotton and outdoors, something distinctively male that I had no problem recognizing, even though it had been years since I smelled it. The fragrance, while very subtle, hit me in the chest like a ton of bricks, stealing all the air from my lungs.

His husky voice spoke from behind me, forcing me to squeeze my eyes shut against the onslaught of pain that lanced through my chest. "I'd tell you to go for the Fritos and bean dip, but you were always a tortilla chips and salsa kind of girl."

I stood like that for several seconds until my body finally decided to cooperate and I was able to breathe again. I moved slowly, turning in place to see the boy who'd crushed my heart six years ago, standing directly behind me. And the sight of him was a complete shock to my system. There was no way of possibly confusing him for a *boy* any longer. He was definitely all man. Hell, even the times I'd been forced to watch him on TV during a game, or stumbled across his photo on the cover of a sports magazine while in a checkout line hadn't prepared me for the full effect of Ethan Prewitt, Football God, all grown up and in the flesh.

He was taller than I remembered... by a lot. His chest was wider, shoulders broader. His once lean frame was packed with muscles that even his t-shirt and jeans weren't able to hide. My eyes scanned down his massive frame of their own accord, catching briefly on the crutches resting under his arm and the brace covering the majority of his left leg.

His golden brown eyes were shaded by the brim of a worn out Denver Wildcats ball cap, making his prom-inent, square jawline and straight nose stand out. As if the chiseled features weren't enough to make most women keel over with excitement, there was the brilliant white smile that slowly spread across his lips. All straight white teeth surrounded by full lips. My heart stuttered and that pain grew more intense the longer I stood there staring.

"Ethan." Despite the riot of emotions I was over-come with, my voice was flat. And I knew he heard it too, because that smile of his began to slip from his handsome face.

"Kiddo," he said in a low voice. "Christ, I've missed you."

That nickname hit me right in the stomach, and my knees threatened to buckle underneath me. I was so overcome with the fear that I was about to hit the ground that I barely had time to register the sound of his crutches hitting the floor. Suddenly two strong arms wrapped around my body, holding me up while squeezing my lungs to the point of discomfort.

The sight of Ethan had caused a short in my brain so bad that it took me several seconds to realize what was happening. Was he...? His head turned and I felt his nose brush my neck as he inhaled deeply. *Sniffing* me.

Oh sweet mother of hell, Ethan was *hugging* me in the middle of Mabel's Corner Market. After six years of radio silence. After having torn me in half with his hateful words.

"Damn, Eliza. It's so fucking good to see you. You have no idea," he whispered against my skin.

Once I realized exactly what was happening, the shock of the situation wore off quickly, and white-hot anger took its place.

My whole body went rigid. "Let. Go," I ground out between clenched teeth.

His body went stiff against me. The steel band of his arms around me loosened as he lifted his head from the crook of my neck.

He was so close now that as he looked down at me, I could see those frowning golden eyes perfectly beneath the bill of his baseball cap. "Eliz—"

I held up my hand to stop him. "No. Just..." What the hell was I actually planning on saying? As each year passed and my anger at Ethan intensified, I'd done what any sane, rational girl did when hurt by one of her best friends who she just so happened to have had a crush on at a young age. I rehearsed exactly what I would say to him if I ever got the chance. I had the whole thing memorized... and it was freaking brilliant. Each sentence was carefully thought out to inflict the most damage. In my imagination, I was dressed to the nines, hair perfect, makeup flawless, and everything I had to say would absolutely *destroy* him.

But in reality? Well, I was wearing the same tank top I'd been cooking in all day, my hair was a ratty mess, thrown up on the top of my head, I sweated my makeup off hours ago, and I was pretty sure I smelled particularly ripe after a day spent in a hot-as-shit kitchen.

And the worst part — I couldn't remember what I spent *years* planning on saying to him. Not a fucking word of it.

The best I could come up with was a whispered, "I have to go," just before dropping my basket on the floor at my feet with a loud clatter.

I tried in vain to tune his voice out as I scurried down the aisle and out of the store with none of the items I intended to buy. Once my feet hit the wood planks of the sidewalk, I broke out into a run, not slowing down until I hit the staircase in the alley behind Sinful Sweets that led up to my apartment.

My hands were so shaky by the time I reached the landing that I dropped my keys three times before finally getting the door unlocked. Once I stepped inside, I slammed it behind me and hunched over, hands to knees, completely out of breath.

"What the hell?" Lilly said, coming around the corner from the living room. "You look like you just saw a ghost. What's going on? And where's the junk food and wine?"

"E-Ethan," I panted, sucking in as much air as possible.

Her face twisted in confusion. "*Ethan?* Ethan what?"

"He... the store... hugged me... ran away..." Dear God, I was really out of shape. I gulped in more air. "Bastard... made me... do cardio... I hate him."

"Was anything you just said supposed to make

actual sense? Are you drunk right now? Is that what's going on?"

Once I could finally breathe again, I straightened and leaned back against the door, shooting her a dead glare for good measure. "No, I'm not drunk. Ethan's here. I ran into him at the corner store."

Her eyes grew so big I worried they might just pop out. "He's here? Like *here,* here? As in Pembrooke here?"

Okay, so I might have failed to mention to my best friend that my *other* best friend — the one I currently hated with the fire of a thousand suns —had moved back indefinitely, but in my defense... well, she probably would have tracked him down and broken his *other* knee for hurting me. Lilly was kind of fierce like that.

"He's back at Harlow and Noah's place."

"*What?!*" she shrieked. "Are you kidding me? And you just found out?"

I managed a guilty grimace as I shrugged noncommittally. "Well..."

"Oh *hell no*! You've known about this and didn't tell me?!"

I threw my arms out at my sides, ready to beg forgiveness. "I'm sorry! But if you think about it, I did you a favor by keeping it a secret."

Lilly crossed her arms over her chest and scowled. "Oh really? And how do you figure that?"

I pushed off the door and started for the kitchen, hoping against hope that the secret bottle of wine I kept stashed for emergency purposes was still in its hiding spot. "You're not currently locked up for attempted murder, are you? You're welcome." Standing on my tiptoes, I reached for the cabinet high above the fridge. I had to strain to reach, but once the cool glass of the bottle hit my fingers, I sighed in relief.

"And you hide wine from me, too?!" Lilley shouted in outrage. "What kind of friendship is this? I feel like I don't even know you anymore."

"Stop pouting," I scolded as I rummaged in the drawer for our corkscrew. "I totally intend on sharing. I just need about a glass of this before I do." The popping sound of the cork was like music to my ears. I brought the bottle to my lips and took a huge gulp, not bothering with something as tedious as a glass.

Lilly grabbed the bottle from my hand once I'd downed a quarter of it. "Okay, wino. Now that you've had your liquid courage, tell me what's going on."

Deciding the best course of action was to just rip the Band-Aid right off, I dove in, telling her everything Chloe told me the week before, and how I had every intention of just staying away from Ethan until he inevitably headed back to Denver and disappeared off the map for another six years. By the time I reached the part where I ran out of Mabel's like my ass was on fire, she had wisely reached over head and pulled two of our largest wineglasses from the cabinet, filling mine to the very top like the amazing friend she was.

"So, let me get this straight." She paused long enough to take a sip of the red wine. "That prick actually had the balls to tell you he missed you and hug you like it was nothing?"

"Pretty much." Tipping my head back, I drained the contents of my glass and held it out for a refill.

"And instead of laying into his ass like you've been planning to do for the past six years, you ran out of there like a marathoner."

"Yep." I chugged more wine.

"Well," she sighed before draining her own glass, "I'd say you're the winner of Shittiest Day Ever."

Moving from the kitchen into the living room, I plopped down on the couch in a dramatic fashion. "And you know I'm allergic to all things exercise. Running like that could have killed me! And it's all his fault."

Taking a seat at the other end of the couch, Lilly shot me her signature *"Bitch, please"* look. "There's no such thing as being allergic to exercise, Eliza. You're just *really* out of shape."

"You don't know science!" I argued irrationally —

and pathetically, might I add. But after seeing Ethan, I was feeling anything but rational.

"Fine," she said sarcastically. "Ethan's totally to blame for the terrifying brush with death you just had."

"Whatever," I huffed. "Then it's his fault we aren't stuffing our faces with Oreos and Tostitos."

We fell into a thoughtful silence as I laid back on the couch, resting my head on one arm and my feet in Lilly's lap. I'd just about finished off my second — or was it third — glass of wine when she spoke again. "So what are you going to do now?"

And that was the real question, wasn't it? "Aside from becoming a hermit for the foreseeable future, I don't have a clue."

She gave my foot a squeeze. "Well, if you need anything I'm here. And I'm 96.2 percent sure I know how to dispose of a body without being caught."

While that number didn't inspire my utmost faith in her skills, Lilly's offer did solidify one thing.

Ethan Prewitt could suck it. Lilly was the best friend *ever*.

Chapter Six

Ethan

P*ast*

"Hey."

At the sound of Eliza's voice carrying on the soft breeze, I tilted my head away from the darkening sky.

"I've been looking for you."

"How'd you find me?" I asked, ignoring her initial question.

The grass and dried leaves crunched under her shoes as she made her way toward me. "Well, if I were anyone else, I would have probably assumed you were either parked somewhere on Gaslow Lane with a random girl in your back seat or at Patrick Bewler's bonfire party. But seeing as I'm your best friend, it was easy to read your mood when you got home yesterday. Something's upset you, and this is your private place."

"You know," I started, turning back around to face the sunset, "it's not normal for a fifteen year old to be as observant as you are. Shouldn't you be busy thinking about things like makeup and purses or some materialistic shit like that? Sometimes you sound like you're older than me."

She snorted as she lowered herself to the ground beside me, folding her legs in front of her and facing the small cliff we'd stumbled upon a few years ago while hiking the mountain trails around her father's house. It was a small, secluded spot that most people in town didn't know existed, but with what seemed like a never ending view of the tree covered mountains, it was the ideal spot to escape and think. "Not too hard to do, considering you still manage to act like a toddler more times than not." She let out a small laugh. "And according to the state, you'll be old enough to legally drink starting next month. How's that for unfair?"

"Watch it, kiddo. I'd hate for you to 'accidentally' take a tumble over the side there," I said in mock warning, causing her to grin at me. "And what the hell are you doing out here by yourself anyway?" I finally asked, that big brother instinct I had when it came to Eliza in full effect. I loved my sister and her daughter Lucy with all the breath in my body, but the protectiveness I felt for my best friend was unlike anything I'd experienced with anyone else. She might as well have been raised as my sister with the way I hovered over her the past few years, keeping dipshit boys away and making sure she was safe whenever her father wasn't around to do it. "It's almost dark, Eliza. It's not safe. You know your dad would lose his fucking mind if he knew you were wandering the woods by yourself at sunset."

She rolled her eyes before laying on her back and staring up at the darkening sky. "Would you relax, Over Protective? He knows where I am. I told him I figured you were out here, and he knows you're just as likely to shoot someone in my defense as he is."

"Damn straight," I grumbled, making her laugh.

"I'm pretty sure if he could pay you for your bodyguard services, he would."

I looked over at her and smiled my first genuine smile in what felt like days. "Wouldn't need to. I'm all too happy to go big brother on anyone's ass who needs it."

"So," she leaned over to bump my shoulder with hers, "you going to tell me what's got you sitting out in the middle of nowhere all introspective when you should be enjoying your Spring Break, college boy?"

"Introspective," I repeated with a laugh. "Someone's been hitting her SAT books."

"Well not all of us can get into college on a football scholarship. It's academics or bust for me. And stop trying to change the subject. It's not going to work. You know better."

I let out a defeated sigh knowing there was no way she was going to give in. "It's nothing. I'm just in a funk, I guess." The look on her face told me she knew I was full of shit, so I sighed again and finally relented. "It's just getting harder and harder to come back every time," I admitted.

"What? Why? This is your home, everyone you love is here."

I had to turn away from the frown marring her face. There was no way to say what I was feeling without offending her. She would take it personally, even though I didn't mean it that way.

"I don't know. This place just doesn't really feel like home anymore. Hasn't for a while if I'm being honest. Harlow has Noah, and they've got their own little family. You know I've felt out of place since my Gram died," I said, bringing up a painful point I'd talked with her about more than once over the years. "I've felt like an outsider for a really long time. And now that I'm away at college, it's just becoming more and more obvious."

Sure enough, Eliza's face looked like I just smacked her. It only added to the guilt already resting on my shoulders for feeling the way I did. "But... they're your family. *We're* your family. You know that. Maybe if you talked to Harlow and Noah—"

"And say what?" I interrupted with a sarcastic bark of laughter before taking on a mocking tone. "'Hey guys, I know you're all in love and shit, but when I look at you, it makes me realize that I'm the third-fucking-wheel in our family, so can you maybe tone down on the happiness for a while so I don't feel so out of place'? Come on, Eliza. Be realistic. I'm selfish enough even feeling this way. Saying it out loud just makes it a thousand times worse."

"It's not selfish," she insisted, her voice trembling with vehemence. "You lost your parents before you were even old enough to really remember them, then your older sister just took off on you for years. The one stable person you had for any extended period of time died, and when Harlow finally came back, she automatically jumped into a relationship with Noah and they had a baby. It's not selfish to feel like an outsider. I don't blame you. I just think that if you *talked* to them—"

I cut her off again, even though everything she'd just

said was spot-fucking-on. "I'm not going to do that, Eliza. Just stop pushing it, okay?"

We both remained quiet as the sun finally finished its descent, leaving us with nothing but millions of tiny little stars as the only light to see by. I wanted to tell her that she was the only person who made me feel like I belonged, that even though Harlow was my sister by blood, the bond I had with Eliza was stronger. I wanted to tell her how I dreamed of leaving and never coming back, of starting a life for myself somewhere else, and that she's the only person in this town I'd be willing to stick around for, that she was the best friend I've ever had or probably ever *would* have.

But I didn't. I didn't say any of that.

Instead, I said, "It's late. We should go."

I didn't need to see the disappointment on her face to know it was there... or to feel the full impact of it in the pit of my stomach.

I had just let down one of the most important people in my life, and that killed worse than anything else.

Chapter Seven

Ethan

I DON'T KNOW how long I stood staring at the basket lying on the ground where Eliza had abandoned it, but it was long enough for my knee to start protesting the slight weight I put on it after dropping my crutches in order to hug her.

"Shit," I muttered to myself, leaning down to grab my discarded crutches. I put them under my arms and began to turn when something near my foot caught my eye. Reaching back over, I scooped up the contents Eliza had dropped to the floor and threw them back in the basket. Two packages of mega stuffed Oreo's and a box of some churro things that looked pretty damned good if I did say so myself.

When I found her, she'd been scoping out chips and dip. It might have been years since I had seen or talked to her, but I still knew her well enough to know the girl — well, *woman* now — was a massive junk food junkie. And because of me, she'd stormed out without her fix.

I lifted the basket the best I could while trying to balance it and my crutches at the same time as I scanned the shelves in front of me. A plan was taking form in my brain as I spotted a jar of salsa I'd seen Eliza eat a ton of times growing up. I put it in the basket with the rest of the junk food, along with a bag of tortilla chips, and headed for the register.

"Well, I'll be," Mabel said as I lifted the basket onto the counter and began unloading it. "If it isn't our very own football star. It's been a long time, Ethan. How have you been?"

The *'football star'* thing grated on my nerves. Especially now that I was out for the whole fucking season. Tipping the brim of my ball cap up in order to see her clearly, I offered a small smile that didn't come close to reaching my eyes. "I'm good, Ms. Mabel. How about you?"

Her eyes trailed over what she could see of my frame from behind the counter as she scanned my purchases. "Better now." The creepy grin the plump old woman gave me probably would have made lesser men run in fear. I couldn't lie, I'd always been leery around Mabel, mindful to never stand too close or run the risk of getting certain parts of my body fondled. The woman had a knack for sneaking up on a poor, unsuspecting guy and grabbing his junk before he knew what the hell was happening. I'd been on the receiving end of such treatments more than once.

"Mmm mmm," she hummed appreciatively. However, I'd grown used to her over the years, so the hairs on the back of my neck no longer stood on end. "You sure did grow up fine, didn't you, honey?"

"And you're just as beautiful as ever," I replied, giving her a wink.

Her wrinkled cheeks grew a deep shade of red as she waved me off and giggled like a teenager. "Oh, you. So shameless."

"That's me." I watched her fingers as she hit a few buttons on the register, lost in thought until she spoke.

"So... you getting this for Eliza Anderson?" My head gave a startled jerk up to find her staring back at me with a knowing smile stretched across her face. She didn't bother waiting for me to respond before continuing. "I saw that pretty little Eliza take off like a bat outta hell, looking all kinds of mad. You two used to be close friends, didn't you?"

"Yes," I answered at a near growl, feeling my brows pull down into a deep frown at the woman's nosiness.

"And, if my old mind is recalling correctly, you haven't been back home in quite some time, have you?"

"And I don't recall you ever being one to beat around the bush," I stated, already over the back and forth she seemed to be getting off on. "Why don't you just go ahead and say what's on your mind?"

Her head fell back with a cheerful laugh before she surprised me by walking around the counter and passing me on the way to a wine display set up about fifteen feet away. She came back, still smiling with humor before ringing the bottle up and recalculating my purchases. "You're going to need *that* if you're hoping to get back into her good graces any time soon, boy." She held up the bottle and gave it a little wave before bagging it and the rest of the items in a canvas bag. "That'll be fifty-two fifty. Normally I'd have grabbed a cheaper bottle of wine. But you're a professional football player with two Super Bowl rings. I figured you could afford the good stuff."

She slid the bag toward me as I reached into my wallet and pulled out a couple bills. Little did she know I'd been known to drop three times as much on a bottle of bourbon.

"Keep the change," I said, trying and failing to keep my smirk at bay. The damn woman used to be a handful on a good day, and seeing as that hadn't changed in the past six years was a little refreshing — beneath the skin-crawling creepiness of being hit on by a senior citizen that used to get off on grabbing dicks, that is.

Some things never changed, and Mabel would stay the same until the day she died. I wasn't sure why, maybe it was because I was hoping it would be the same with Eliza, but that realization gave me a tiny sense of comfort.

Slinging the handles of the canvas bag over my shoulder, I started hobbling my way toward the store's entrance, my sole focus, getting to Eliza with a bag full of her favorite stuff that would hopefully make headway in getting her to forgive me.

I was almost there when something hit me. I looked over my shoulder. "Uh, Mabel?"

"Yes?"

I gave her a sheepish smile. "You wouldn't happen to know where she lives, would you?"

Mabel slow blinked for several seconds before asking, "Ran off any boy within a ten-mile radius of the girl most of her teenage years, and you didn't even bother to keep up with where she lives?"

All I could do was shrug as her chastisement pierced right through my chest. I really had been a shitty friend to her. It wasn't as though she could have controlled how things changed in my mind. Hell, she didn't even have a clue. It was no wonder she took off rather than talk to me earlier. "It's been a while," was all I could come up with in response.

"She lives in the apartment over the café." She huffed with irritation before muttering to herself — loud enough for me to hear, "Lord blessed the boy with looks, but made him dumb as a box of rocks," as she turned away.

I took that as a sign and escaped the Corner Store relatively unscathed after a run-in with the owner. The rubber bottoms of my crutches thumped softly on the wooden walkway as I passed storefront after storefront. The trek took longer than usual, thanks to my bum knee, but it gave me the time to think up a plan to get myself back into Eliza's good graces. And after that first brief glimpse of her on the sidewalk earlier, I knew I *had* to get back there. Just one look and I felt the loss of her like a physical thing crushing down on me.

I missed her like crazy.

And God, did she look good. From our exchange in the store, I knew that the teenage girl I knew before I left was long gone. I never doubted she'd grow up to be beautiful, she was beautiful as a girl, but I was stunned at the change six years could bring.

It was like looking at a stranger. And thinking about it, I realized she *was* a stranger. The familiarity in those beautiful hazel eyes of hers was absent when I'd looked into them. I had a feeling that earning her trust back was going to take a hell of a lot more than a simple *"I'm sorry."*

With that realization, I decided it was best if I just left the bag of groceries on her doorstep with a note. Maybe that would thaw her out enough to allow me a chance to apologize face to face.

Rounding the building that housed the expanded Sinful Sweets and a dance studio that hadn't been there when I'd left Pembrooke, I found the back stairs that led to the landing of the upstairs apartment. That was when I realized I hadn't really thought this out. Because getting up those steps was going to be a bitch and a half.

"Fuck," I mumbled to myself as I tried to figure out the best way to maneuver the stairs. I finally decided it would be best to only use one crutch. It took longer than it should to get to the top, and by the time I made it, my knee ached and I'd tripped on at least two of the steps, nearly losing the bag of groceries along the way. I released a relieved sigh once I finally made it to the top, followed quickly by a "Goddamn it," when I realized I didn't have a pen or piece of paper to leave a note. I quickly spun around to look for anything I could use, and immediately sent the leg of my crutch crashing into one of the planters that sat on the minuscule landing. I winced and froze as the loud sound of the terra-cotta pot breaking echoed through the otherwise silent night.

I was just about to bolt — knee be damned — when the porch light flipped on and the front door swung open.

"Ethan? What the hell are you doing?"

My mouth opened to answer, but the words died in my throat at the sight of Eliza standing in the open doorway wearing nothing but silky blue pajamas. The spaghetti strap top did nothing to conceal her boobs — which were obviously much bigger than I remembered them being — and the shorts were barely long enough to cover her ass.

Her hair was wet, hanging down around her shoulders, causing the sorry excuse for a shirt to turn damn near transparent. The most disturbing thing about the sight of Eliza, all grown up and looking gorgeous, was that I actually felt my cock begin to stir behind the zipper of my jeans. My feelings for her were definitely changing by the time I left, but standing there just then, I experienced something completely different, the desire so strong, so carnal, it was almost impossible to keep it in check.

It was as if all the blood in my body rushed to that particular region, leaving my brain deprived. That was the only excuse I had for the words that came out of my mouth next.

"That's what you wear to answer the door?!" I yelled. "You're practically naked!"

The confusion that had been on her beautiful face just seconds ago instantly morphed into anger. She crossed her arms over her full, luscious — *Christ, Ethan! Get your shit together!* — breasts and scowled so hard I thought she was trying to set me on fire with her mind.

"I'm not naked, you asshole," she bit back. "And the only reason I opened the door like this was because I thought you were someone trying to break in!"

I was pretty sure my brain exploded with that statement. Every single protective instinct I ever had when it came to her reared back up to the surface. "You thought I was an intruder so you *opened the door?!* What the fuck, Eliza! Your dad's the Sheriff, for Christ's sake, you know better! I have half a mind to call Derrick and let him know you're just asking to be raped and murdered."

"Don't you dare! You have no right, Ethan. You're not my brother. You're not even my *friend*! You can't just blow back into town after six years and act like nothing's changed!"

"When it comes to your wellbeing, I'll do whatever the fuck I have to, to make sure you're safe!"

"Stop yelling at me!" she shouted back before

sucking in a deep breath and taking a step back, running her hands through her damp hair in obvious frustration. It made her tits stick out further and strain against her top. It took all the willpower I had to pull my eyes from the amazing view. I was pretty sure there was a special place in Hell just for me.

Fortunately, her momentary silence gave me the opportunity I needed to pull my mind out of the gutter and screw my head on straight. I was there to try and win my best friend back. I wasn't going to be able to do that by yelling at her and staring at her tits like they were the first pair I'd ever seen.

I sighed running a hand over my face. "I'm sorry I yelled at you."

Her glare remained firmly in place as she ignored my apology and demanded to know, "What are you even doing here?"

Balancing on the one crutch, I leaned down, grabbed the grocery bag and held it out to her. "You dropped this stuff on the way out. I know what a junk food fiend you are, so I figured you'd want it."

Hesitantly taking the bag from my hands, she pulled the handles open and peeked inside. Her brows lowered, but this time, in confusion, not anger. Or at least that was what I hoped. She turned those amazing hazel eyes back to me. "You bought this?"

I shrugged and gave her a small smile in response. Eliza reached into the bag and pulled out the jar of salsa that I'd picked on my own. "I remembered that used to be your favorite. I wasn't sure..." I trailed off, not wanting to finish that sentence and draw even *more* attention to the fact that I didn't know her the way I used to.

"It still is," she whispered, her eyes trained on the jar before she dropped it back inside and looked up. "And the wine?"

"I guess you could look at it as an apology."

Her head dropped as she cleared her throat. She refused to meet my gaze again as she spoke quietly. "Well, thanks... I guess."

"You're welcome," I said softly, hoping she'd look at me again and feeling bereft when she simply turned around and went back inside without giving me another glance with those eyes before shutting the door on me.

I carefully made my way down the stairs knowing one thing for absolute certain.

I had my work cut out for me.

Chapter Eight

Eliza

MY HEAD HAD been throbbing for the past two days.

That was why, as I drove up the long, tree-lined driveway that led to my father and Chloe's house further up in the mountain, I dreaded being summoned to a family dinner. I'd suffered from migraines all my life. Fortunately, they were infrequent, but they were bad enough that I knew the signs that pointed to the throbbing behind my eyes being more than just a standard headache.

And I was pretty certain the current throb in my head was about to get much, *much* worse before it got better. The tiny, nagging pain started shortly after I closed my apartment door on Ethan the other night, and it had only gotten subtly worse as the days progressed.

The only saving grace after that epically disastrous exchange was the fact that Lilly slept like the dead through the whole thing, so I didn't have to deal with her rapid-fire questions.

The moment my car pulled to a stop in front of the house the front door flew open and my sisters Cate and Abbi came bounding down the front walk, pushing and shoving at each other like getting to me first was some sort of competition. Sure enough, poor Abbi's hair was several inches shorter than it had been the last time I saw her. Luckily, she was only five, and adorable, so the terrible haircut could be overlooked.

"Hey munchkins!" I kneeled down, ignoring the pain in my head in order to give my sisters a great big hug. "I've missed you guys!"

"We missed you too!" Abbi exclaimed before Cate added, "You should come see us more. Daddy says he never should've let you move out on your own. Now you never come home."

"Of course he did." I grinned, knowing full well my father had put that particular guilt trip in Cate's head because he knew she couldn't keep a secret to save her life. That was his passive-aggressive way of letting me know he was *not* happy with my once a week visits.

Out of the corner of my eye, I saw Chloe coming out of the house and slowly making her way in our direction. I looked up to give her a smile, only to have it fall when I saw the worry on her face. I'd just opened my mouth to ask what was wrong when Abbi jerked on my hand.

"Guess what! Guess what!"

"What?" I asked, tipping my head down at her.

"Aunt Harlow and Uncle Noah are coming to dinner! And they're bringing Lucy and Evan! It's gonna be so fun!"

Suddenly I knew exactly why Chloe had looked so concerned. My head shot up, my wide eyes hitting hers in question. She knew exactly what I was asking and shrugged in response. She had no clue if Ethan was coming with them or not.

Well shit.

My lips pursed in agitation as I frowned. Clearly having lost interest in their big sister, Cate and Abbi took off back inside the house as I made my way to Chloe.

"I'm sorry, sweetheart. Your dad didn't tell me you were coming over tonight."

With a deep sigh, I tried my best to paste a smile on my face. It wasn't her fault after all. "It's fine. I'm sure he probably won't be with them anyway."

Just then, the sound of a vehicle — or more importantly, *two* vehicles — coming up the drive drew our attention in that direction, and my hope vanished.

"Damn it," I muttered as Chloe breathed a soft, "Oh hell."

I wanted to run and hide, but I knew that would only make me look childish. And I didn't want to give Ethan the satisfaction, so I stood there and held my ground next to my stepmom while the cars came to a stop. I watched on as Harlow climbed from the passenger seat of her car and offered me a hesitant smile. Of course, being Chloe's best friend, she knew all about my pain over her brother's abandonment. Lucky for me, she was in *my* corner.

Harlow stepped in front of us and leaned in to kiss my cheek. "Hey ladies." Then her eyes came directly to me as her voice lowered, "When he heard where we were going, he insisted. Just walked out of the house before I could say a word."

"It's fine," I assured her, even though it *so* wasn't. The loud creak of metal caused my head to snap up just as Ethan climbed down from the old beat up truck he was driving. When his gaze caught mine, he offered a tentative grin. I didn't return the sentiment. Instead, I closed my eyes and reached up to rub my temples as the dull pain turned into a shooting one.

Chloe's soft touch on my arm caught my attention. "You okay?"

"Yeah," I lied. "Just a bit of a headache.

Her brows shot down, forming a deep V over her bright green eyes. She knew I was prone to migraines, but the last thing I needed was for her to worry about me. It would have only added to my stress. "Do you need to take something?"

"I took some Advil just before I headed over here. I'll be good in a few minutes. Don't worry."

She didn't look convinced, but before she could question me further, I was saved by the rest of Harlow's family joining us, with the exception of Evan who ran into the house, no doubt to join Cate and Abbi in something destructive. I adored Harlow's family... well, *most* of them anyway, so I prayed they would be a decent buffer between me and Ethan. Noah pulled me into his side and pressed a small kiss to my temple before releasing me to move on to Chloe. I could feel Ethan's eyes burning into my skin as he joined our little huddle, but I refused to look his way. Thirteen-year-old Lucy mumbled, *"Hey"* in everyone's direction while keeping her eyes glued to her phone, thumbs moving at lightning speed while texting. So maybe I wasn't going to have the buffer I'd hoped for.

"Lucy, what'd I tell you about that damn phone," Noah barked in his 'Dad' voice. In response, Lucy's eyes rolled so far back in her head I worried they'd get stuck that way.

"God, Dad. Chill out. I'm just texting Krista real quick. I'll put it away in a second." She went right back to her phone and commenced texting like her tall, built, intimidating-to-everyone-else-on-the-planet-except-her father hadn't said a word. I had to give it to the girl, she had some balls.

"I swear to Christ," Noah grumbled while swinging his arm around his wife's shoulders. "Pre-teen girls are going to be the death of me. I don't remember you ever being such a massive pain in my ass, Eliza. Maybe you can teach my girl here a few things."

Lucy, unfazed by her father's words, simply snorted and turned to head for the house, eyes still on her phone.

"Eliza was always the exception to the rule," Ethan said in a soft voice, causing my body to go stiff. I wasn't going to look at him. *I wasn't.* But I could hear the reverence in his tone and my stupid eye-balls just wouldn't listen, tipping in his direction against my will. Those honey-colored eyes of his flashed as soon as mine hit them, shining with sincerity that I just couldn't handle at that moment.

"What the hell's everyone standing around the driveway for?" My father's booming voice called from the open front door. I used his appearance as my means of escape, pulling away from our small group to go to him.

"Hey, Daddy." I gave him a genuine smile and stood on my tip-toes to kiss his scowling cheek.

"You don't come home enough," he huffed.

With a laugh, I said, "I just saw you yesterday, old man. Plus, you come to the café for lunch almost every day. And I was here for dinner last week!"

"Still not enough," he grumbled, but he did it, wrapping me in a tight bear hug. There was nothing better than one of my father's hugs. With the exception of heartbreak, they could pretty much mend anything. "I think you should consider moving back in here."

At that all too familiar topic, my head fell back on a groan. "Not again, Dad. We've talked about this a million times."

He opened his mouth to argue, but was cut off by Chloe. I could have kissed the woman. "Leave her alone, Derrick. She's perfectly capable of taking care of herself, and her apartment's only a few minutes away. You're being ridiculous."

Shooting her a murderous glare before turning away, he announced to everyone, "Let's eat!"

As if having dinner with Ethan present wasn't bad enough, he'd taken the seat right across from me so it was damn near impossible to avoid eye contact. And even though I'd somehow managed I could feel his gaze like a tangible thing along my skin. The few times I accidentally looked up, or my curiosity forced me to, he was staring back at me with an expression on his face that I couldn't read.

My belly dipped every time I saw his eyes glimmer, making me hate myself for my reaction. I didn't want to feel anything for him other than disdain. Unfortunately, my body had other ideas. He'd always been attractive. I wasn't blind growing up, but once my childhood crush waned, the obsession with his appearance had fallen to the back burner. However, *grown up* Eliza couldn't help but notice just how fine Ethan had grown up to be.

And *damn*, was that man fine.

My father's voice cut through my head, bringing me back to real time. "So, Ethan, how's the knee feeling?"

I begrudgingly found myself looking in his direction, waiting for his answer. Old Eliza cared about Ethan's wellbeing more than her own. It appeared that was a particularly hard habit to break.

"It's fine. Getting better every day." My chest squeezed uncomfortably, because despite his casual return, I could see the tension tightening the skin around his mouth and eyes. That was something that only I'd been able to read when we were younger, and that still seemed to be the case today.

"He's been doing PT with Fletch and is down to only one crutch," Harlow chirped like he was just days away from being fully healed. Ethan's face grew tighter, telling me just how badly he was handling not being in the game. I knew exactly how much football meant to him and seeing that pain on his face, although masked well, made me sad for him. I didn't *want* to care, but I wasn't a heartless person. I just couldn't help it.

"That's good, son," Dad replied. "We've missed watching you on Sunday's. Next season will be here before you know it."

The fork in Ethan's hand looked like it was seconds away from being bent in half thanks to his white-knuckled grip. I wasn't sure exactly what possessed me to do it, but I found myself speaking up to divert attention. "Noah, how's the high school team looking this year? Sorry I haven't been able to make it to any of the games. Things with the café have been crazy."

The conversation smoothly transitioned from Ethan to Pembrooke High and when my eyes skated past his to return to my plate I couldn't miss the thankful smile he shot my way. I ignored the look and rubbed my head.

The sharp pains in my temples had returned throughout dinner, shooting daggers through my skull at a faster rate. I needed to get away from that table, and fast. My rioting emotions when it came to Ethan, coupled with the screams of the three spawns of Satan at the other end of the table were a recipe for disaster.

"Hey." At the sound of Ethan's insistent voice I had no choice but to look at him. And the concern marring his brow only made the tightness in my chest worse, and added a belly flip for good measure. "You okay?"

"I'm fine," I answered shortly, picking up my fork and stabbing at a piece of roast on my plate. In spite of the fact my stomach was protesting the thought of food, I was more than willing to shovel the rest of my dinner into my mouth if it meant I could get out of there faster.

"You don't look fine," he continued to push. "You're really pale, kiddo."

Now it was *my* fork in danger of being bent in half. "He's right, baby girl," my father spoke carefully from beside me at the head of the table. "You're not looking too good. Is it a migraine?"

I clenched my eyes shut and nodded. I had no choice but to tell the truth. That damned incessant pain in my head wasn't going to let up. With each passing minute, it was growing closer and closer to becoming unbearable. I pulled in a deep breath and pushed up from my chair, holding on to the edge of the table for balance. "I need to get home before it's so bad I can't drive."

My father shot up and wrapped his arm around my waist, holding me to his side so he could take most of my weight. "Like hell you do. You aren't driving like this, Eliza. You can stay here tonight."

"And sleep where?" I asked with a chuckle, immediately wincing when the noise sliced through my head. "Dad, I need dark and quiet. I love all of you more than anything, but you have to admit, that's not something I can get here."

He looked like he wanted to argue but didn't seeing as I was totally right.

"I'll take her home."

My eyes went wide at Ethan's declaration. "Good idea, son," Dad spoke up. Noah nodded in agreement. Son of a bitch. Neither of them knew about what went down between me and Ethan. Men were so freaking clueless it was painful.

I was just about to protest when Harlow jumped into the fray, bless her heart. "Oh, you don't have to. I'll take her home."

"Wildflower, you've had two glasses of wine already," Noah pointed out, earning himself a killing look from his wife. He looked startled. Poor guy had no clue what he'd just done to earn her wrath.

"Then I'll take her." Chloe stood from her chair and began to move my way.

"That doesn't make sense, sunshine," Dad argued. "You'd have to go there and come back. If Ethan takes her, he can stay to make sure she's okay, and Noah and Harlow can just swing by to pick him up on their way home."

I watched with growing panic as Harlow and Chloe's faces fell in defeat. My father's argument was just too solid. Sometimes I really hated his stupid cop brain.

"That settles it," Ethan spoke, standing from the table and grabbing the one crutch. He reached into the pocket of his jeans — jeans which fit him *really* well, I'd unfortunately noticed — and pulled out a set of keys, tossing them to my dad. "I'm moving a little slower these days. You mind getting her into my truck, Derrick?"

Dad caught the keys and all but carried me out of the house.

And just like that, thanks to my traitorous head, I was forced to spend alone time with the enemy.

Chapter Nine

Ethan

SEEING ELIZA IN so much pain twisted my gut into painful knots that only squeezed tighter with every pained moan or whimper that came from her as we made the drive to her apartment. Maneuvering her up the steps was a definite struggle, but I somehow managed to get her up, and find her keys in her purse without jostling her too much. It was once we got inside that things became more difficult.

"What's going on?" I looked from where I held Eliza close to my side toward the woman standing from the couch. "Holy shit. Ethan?"

"Lilly?" I asked the blonde standing in front of us who looked somewhat familiar. I'd only met her a couple of times back in the day. She was one of Eliza's closest friends, but she'd lived in Jackson Hole so I didn't see her all that often.

"What the hell happened?" she asked, rushing to Eliza and cupping her cheeks.

"Migraine," Eliza answered in a small voice. "Just need one of my pills and sleep. I'll be okay." She sounded far from okay, and just hearing that ripped at my heart.

"Oh, babe," Lilly mumbled. "Okay. I'll take care of it." To my surprise, she moved to my girl's other side and tried pulling her from my arms. "I got her, Ethan. You can go now."

"What?"

The look she gave me was anything but friendly. "I said you can go. I'll take care of her."

Something proprietary coursed through my veins at her sharp words, and I found myself holding tighter to Eliza. She was *mine*. "Like hell I'm leaving. *I'll* take care of her."

Lilly's face pinched up in distaste. "She doesn't need you. You've already caused enough damage. Just leave. Let someone who actually *cares* about her take care of her."

My eyes widened as anger began to simmer in my blood. "You think I don't care about her?"

"I think you've already proven just how much you

care," she scoffed and pulled at Eliza. "Just let her go. This isn't going to win you any brownie points."

I tugged her back against me. "Fuck that," I growled. "I fucking care, and I'm not going anywhere." Oh, if she only knew just *how much* I cared about Eliza.

The two of us were in a standoff so intense that neither of us noticed Eliza's whimpers. "Jesus!" Lilly snapped. "How selfish can you be? Just leave her alone." She gave another tug.

"I'm. Not. Leaving," I ground out.

We instantly stopped struggling when Eliza's pained voice croaked, "I'm going to be sick."

"Shit," Lilly breathed.

Eliza lurched, trying to get away, but I refused to let go. Holding most of her weight, I dropped my crutch and began leading her to the bathroom down the hall. We managed to make it just seconds before she lost the entire contents of her stomach in the toilet.

That tightening in my own stomach returned as I held her hair in one hand, using the other to rub soothing circles on her back as she heaved and groaned at the same time. "Shh. It's okay, sweetheart." I tried my best to comfort her, all the while feeling like the biggest shit for not being able to take her pain away.

Once she was finished, I helped her to the sink to rinse her mouth and all but carried her into what I hoped was her bedroom, so consumed with taking care of her that I hadn't even noticed the pain in my knee. I just wanted to make her better. In that moment, I'd have given anything to make her better. I pulled the covers back and helped ease her in. Not wanting to be far from her, I climbed into the bed, resting my back against the headboard and shifted so that her head was in my lap.

"Here." Lilly rushed into the room with a glass of water and a pill in her hand. "I have your migraine pill, sweetie. I need you to sit up and take it for me. It'll just take a second, can you do that?"

"Yeah," she whispered, coming up on one elbow, eyes still clenched closed.

Once she finished, she laid her head back on my thigh with a sigh. Lilly disappeared for a few minutes before coming back with a damp washcloth that she rested across Eliza's forehead. While she was gone, I'd been running my fingers through Eliza's hair, memorizing the soft, silky feel of it. Her body eventually loosened and her breathing evened out, and I knew she was asleep. Lilly looked like she wanted to rip my head off with her bare hands but was holding back because her friend finally seemed to be comfortable. "I don't like this," she whispered. "I think you're an asshole, but she's comfortable right now so I'm going to let it slide."

"Big of you," I grumbled back defensively, even though I knew I really had no right to be defensive.

"But so help me God, Prewitt, if you hurt her again, missing one season is going to be the *least* of your worries."

My jaw ticked as I clenched my teeth so tight I was surprised one of them didn't break. "I won't," I finally answered. What I didn't say was that I couldn't hurt her again. Because there was no way I'd survive causing Eliza that kind of pain for a second time. Living without her for six years was like walking around with a missing limb. Now that I'd returned, I knew there was no way I could go back to that existence.

With one last glare, she headed for the door, shut off the bedroom light, and pulled the door closed behind her, leaving me alone with the biggest regret of my life. I managed to settle myself enough to prop my injured knee and pulled my cellphone from my pocket.

Me: *Don't pick me up. I'm staying here tonight.*

My sister took less than a minute to respond.

Harlow: *I don't think that's a good idea.*

I felt my jaw clench again.

Me: *Wasn't asking your opinion, sis. I'm staying here. She's not okay, and I'm not leaving her.*

Her following response made my gut clench again

and my chest squeeze so tight it felt like someone's fist was wrapped around it.

Harlow: *She wasn't okay after you left the first time. None of us were. But don't make her go through that again.*

I shoved my phone into my pocket without replying. I didn't think I could have possibly felt any worse than I already had, but picturing Eliza hurting and crushed after leaving her behind six years ago killed more than anything I'd ever experienced. Shifting down in the bed, I pulled Eliza more firmly against me until her whole body was fitted against my side. She mumbled incoherently and snuggled deeper, making my insides warm. One of my arms instinctively wrapped firmly around her, holding her in place as if I was afraid she'd disappear.

Everything about her, the warm, soft curves of her body pressed against me, the softness of her hair as I continued to run my fingers through it, the subtle smell of her, something like vanilla and almonds, it all hit me with the force of a Mack truck. Yes, I'd missed her like crazy. I made a huge mistake in throwing her away years ago, but something about this... now... it felt different. The fear I'd experienced at discovering I was falling for my best friend... my *sixteen*-year-old best friend, was gone. She was an adult now, so it was like those mental blocks I'd thrown up years ago had come crashing to the ground.

I couldn't remember ever feeling the way about Eliza that I felt as I lay there in her bed, surrounded by her intoxicating scent. I wasn't a stranger to lust and attraction. I'd had my fair share of plenty since being drafted into the NFL. It was amazing how many women threw themselves at pro football players. But what I was feeling for Eliza just then was stronger than anything I'd ever felt for another woman.

And fuck if that didn't make me feel like the world's biggest asshole.

Because I'd thrown it all away.

AT SOME POINT IN THE MIDDLE OF THE NIGHT, MY bladder woke me up from the most comfortable sleep I'd had in years. The last thing I wanted to do was untangle my and Eliza's bodies, but nature called, and a grown ass man, pissing her bed wasn't something I thought she'd take too kindly to.

I slid gently from the bed, not wanting to wake her, and slowly made my way to the bathroom. My knee throbbed like a bitch as I made my way across the hall and used the bathroom. I rummaged around the medicine cabinet for some ibuprofen, knowing if I didn't take something, I'd feel it even worse in the morning. When I came up empty, I decided to check out the kitchen in the hopes they stashed their meds in there. What I hadn't expected was for Lilly to be awake and standing in the kitchen.

"Sneaking out?"

I frowned as I pulled open a cabinet door. "Just looking for some pain meds. Knee's killing me."

She stood silent for several seconds as I rummaged through the cabinets, coming up empty. Finally, with a resounding sigh, she moved to the other side of the space and opened a cabinet, then tossed me a bottle of ibuprofen. "Here. This should help."

"Thanks," I mumbled as I popped the cap and put the bottle to my lips, swallowing three tablets dry.

"Welcome."

We stood there, wrapped in uncomfortable quiet for a few minutes before I finally couldn't take it any longer. "I know I hurt her," I spoke, staring down at the pill bottle in my hands as I peeled back the label with my thumb nail. "I'm not here to do it again, whether you believe that or not. I want to make things right."

She didn't say a word, forcing my gaze to meet hers as she studied me closely. "Can I ask you a question?"

"You've been more than willing to throw your

hostility in my face since I got here. I don't know why you'd start asking permission now," I replied, one corner of my mouth twitching as I tried to suppress a smirk.

"If you hadn't have gotten hurt... if Harlow hadn't dragged your ass back home, would you still have wanted to make things right?" Her question caused my back to grow stiff. All the muscles in my body went rigid. But she wasn't done. "Or is it just a matter of convenience now?"

"I..." I had no fucking clue how to answer that question. From the moment I left, I felt like something was missing from my life. I was unhappy, filling that void with sex and booze to try and dull the ache. I knew exactly what was causing it, but had the injury not happened, had I not returned to Pembrooke, I didn't know how long I would have continued throwing myself into the game in order to have some semblance of peace. I didn't know how long I would have taken to pull my head out of my ass without the unwanted shove given to me.

"Just think on that, and then consider what it really is you want from Eliza. She doesn't deserve for you to screw with her head a second time."

She didn't wait for my response. Turning on her heel, she walked out of the kitchen leaving me with my own, miserable thoughts.

Chapter Ten

Ethan

P *ast*

SHIT. IF DERRICK KNEW WHAT I WAS DOING HE'D kill me.

Then he'd kill Eliza. Hell, *I* wanted to kill Eliza for putting me in this position, but I couldn't have just left her. The moment I heard her voice on the other line, her words slurred and hard to understand, my stomach plummeted.

I came home needing something normal, something familiar to try and decompress from everything happening in my life. College ending, the draft, just... everything. But instead of everything becoming clearer, my head felt more twisted up than before. Everything was fucked, and I had no clue how to fix it.

Because my feelings for Eliza had changed.

If I were being honest with myself, it had been happening for a while now, but I'd refused to acknowledge it. But after this weekend home, there was no more hiding what was happening. Because the closer my future came, the more I started considering throwing it all away. For her. And it scared the absolute fuck out of me.

She was my best friend.

She was like a sister.

She was *sixteen*, for Christ's sake! I couldn't feel this way about her. I just *couldn't*. It was wrong on so many goddamned levels it wasn't even funny. I'd even gone so far as trying to put a little distance between us, but each and every time my phone rang, I jumped to answer. I just couldn't help myself.

The sight of the massive bonfire before me pulled me from my thoughts. Cars were parked all over the place, kids were everywhere and my chest tightened at the thought of Eliza, drunk, being out here and vulnerable for anyone to take advantage of.

I threw the truck into park and shoved the door

open, not wasting the time it took to pull the keys from the ignition before jumping out of the cab. Every second it took for me to get to Eliza was a second something bad could happen.

I wasn't thinking rationally. I'd been a rebellious teenager myself, after all. God knew how many parties I'd snuck out to attend. But this was different. This was *her*. And if anything happened, if she got hurt in any way, I'd lose my mind.

I'd just started to worry that I wouldn't be able to find her in the massive sea of teenagers when I heard her loud, piercing "Ethan!" over the music.

I didn't hesitate getting to her. I was across the field and at her side in second. I didn't even take in the people all around me as I grabbed hold of her hand and started dragging her behind me.

"Wait, shlow down," she slurred, her feet stumbling beneath her as she tried to keep up. I didn't slow. Instead I scooped her up in my arms and carried her the rest of the way to my truck.

"What were you thinking, coming out here? You could have been hurt!" I snapped once I had her buckled into the passenger seat.

"I was fine," she drawled, her pretty hazel eyes glassy from the beer. "Was havin' fun, s'all."

I glared down at her and slammed the door before

rounding the hood and climbing in. I threw the truck in reverse and hit the gas so hard dirt and dead grass spit up from the tires. "You mad a'me?" she asked after several seconds of silence.

I took a calming breath in through my nose and blew it out on a long exhale. "No," I answered honestly. "I'm not mad. I was worried out of my mind. When you called me drunk and told me where you were, I just about lost it."

"Aw." I could hear the smile in her voice as I kept my eyes on the road. "My bes frien's worried 'bout me." She reached over and gave my shoulder a shove. "Sorry I scared you," she said still drunk, but sounding genuine nonetheless. "Din't mean to."

Her hand came across the center console and landed on mine, her fingers squeezing tight. "Please don' be mad at me."

I turned my palm up and tightened my fingers around hers. "I'm not mad."

"Good," she sighed. From the corner of my eyes I saw her head fall back on the head rest. Her eyes closed as she mumbled, "You're my bes' frien' Ethan. I love you."

That fear came back full force. Because in that very moment I knew exactly what I was going to have to do.

And I hated it with all my heart. Even thinking about it crushed me.

But I had no choice. There was only one solution.

Because I knew in that very moment, without a shred of doubt... I was in love with Eliza.

And it couldn't have been more wrong.

Chapter Eleven

Eliza

P*ast*

I SAT AMONGST THE CROWD IN THE MASSIVE auditorium with my father and Chloe at my sides as I cheered when Ethan walked across the stage. Happy tears filled my eyes and coursed down my cheeks as Harlow, Noah, and Lucy stood beside him, beaming at the cameras while Ethan held up a Denver Wildcats jersey.

He was the only person in the history of Pembrooke to be drafted into the NFL. It was his lifelong dream, and I couldn't have been prouder of him. But at the same time joy spread through my chest, that nagging sense of unease still sat in the pit of my stomach.

Ethan had been uncharacteristically distant for weeks. Ever since the last time he came home. I knew it was hard for him to come back on the weekends since he was in his last year of college, and with the draft coming up, he was under an insane amount of stress. I understood that. What I had trouble understanding was the fact that he hadn't answered or returned a single one of my calls or text messages in three and a half weeks. I would have been lying if I didn't admit that part of the reason I was so excited to have been invited today was so that I'd finally have a chance to talk to my best friend.

Anticipation made my skin prickle as Chloe, Dad, and I stood around the emptying auditorium once the draft was over, waiting for Harlow and her family to come out and join us. I was so antsy it felt like the only thing holding me together was my skin. Dad and Chloe chatted about how amazing it was to have someone so close to us entering the pros, but I couldn't focus on what they were saying. I was too busy scanning the thinning crowd, looking over heads, trying to find that one person I couldn't wait to see.

Finally, after what felt like an eternity, Noah, Harlow, and Lucy came to join us. My stomach clenched when I noticed Ethan wasn't with them, but I hadn't given up hope.

"So where's our boy?" Dad asked once they'd reached us. "I'm starving. Let's get this celebration started." Chloe smacked him playfully in the chest.

Harlow's smile fell slightly and my heart stuttered. "He's not going to be able to make dinner. I didn't realize he'd be so tied up doing interviews and meetings with the coaches and stuff."

"He's not coming?" I finally spoke. My voice cracked a little and that hope I'd been holding on to plummeted. I knew, deep down, that something was seriously wrong with Ethan. I just didn't have a clue what it was. It wasn't like him to not confide in me.

Harlow looped her arm through mine and pulled me along as she started out of the auditorium. "I'm sorry, honey. He really wanted to, he just couldn't get away. But we'll have fun without him."

I let my family and their friends lead me away, all the while thinking that what Harlow said wasn't the full truth.

NERVES HAD TAKEN ROOT IN MY BELLY AS THE phone rang against my ear. The draft had come and gone. Ethan still hadn't returned home, and the last I heard, he'd already purchased an apartment in Denver and hired movers to pack his stuff up at his sister's house and cart it to Colorado. He had no intentions of coming back. And the worst part was, I still hadn't talked to him. So I'd taken measures to ensure he answered my call.

"'Lo," his groggy voice filled the line and just the sound of it caused a lump to form in my throat so big I thought it would choke me. "Hello," he repeated, his voice edged with agitation.

"Ethan?"

Lilly sat across from me on my bed with wide eyes, "He answered?" she mouthed. I waved her off, too busy focusing on the person on the other line.

"Eliza? What number are you calling me from?"

"It's my friend Lilly's phone," I answered flatly.

"Why are you calling from someone else's phone? What happened to yours?" At the sharp, impatient tone of his voice, I felt my anger beginning to rise. "Nothing happened to it," I snapped. "I'm calling you from someone else's phone because you've been avoiding my calls and texts for over *a month,* and I want to know why, Ethan."

He sighed through the line, sounding like he had better things to do than sit on the phone with me. "I don't have time to play your games, Eliza. I've got shit to do. I haven't answered because I'm busy. Ever think of that?"

I didn't want to cry, I really didn't. It made me feel like an immature little kid, but I couldn't help it. "What the hell's going on with you, Ethan? Are you mad at me or something?"

"Jesus, Eliza!" he bit out so harshly it startled me. "Not everything's about you. I'm a grown man who just got drafted into the NFL for Christ's sake. I have responsibilities. I don't have the time to hold your hand whenever your feelings get hurt."

Lilly's face was a mask of worry as she watched me. My jaw clenched and I spoke through my tears, "You don't need to be an asshole."

He let out a loud breath, like he was struggling for patience, "You're just a kid. I wouldn't expect you to understand what it was like in the *adult* world." I inhaled sharply as the pain lanced through me. He'd never, in all our years as friends, thrown my age in my face. I might have only been sixteen to his twenty-two, but I hadn't *felt* like a kid since my own mom taught me what it was like not to be wanted. "Look, I don't have the time for this shit, okay? The fact is, you're a kid, I'm an adult, and things change. The way my life is now, I don't have room for some immature little girl who doesn't have the first clue what the real world is like and will probably be stuck in that po-dunk little town for the rest of her life. I have bigger plans. You just need to move on. Go hang out with people your own age."

I couldn't get enough air in my lungs. My chest physically *ached* as tear after tear fell from my eyes. It wasn't until that very second that I realized just how stupid I was to actually think Ethan cared about me, was ever really my friend.

"I *hate* you," I hissed through clenched teeth with every ounce of feeling inside me. I hit the end button and broke into choking sobs while Lilly held my head in her lap and rubbed my hair.

Chapter Twelve

Eliza

A TICKLING SENSATION along my shoulder woke me from the most restful sleep I'd had in ages. Just like after every migraine, my head felt foggy and it took me a few seconds to get my bearings. Several seconds passed before I realized what the cause of the tickling, as well as the immense heat warming me from chest to toes, was.

And once I figured it out, my entire body went stiff.

"Morning," Ethan's thick, sleep rough voice sent vibrations through his chest straight into mine. Because in my sleep, not only had he managed to climb into bed with me, but I was pressed so close to him we were practically fused together. He was on his back, one arm tucked beneath me and curling around so that he held my entire front to his side. And even thought I kept telling myself I hated him, there was no denying just how muscular he was, if the chest my head was currently resting on, and the thighs my own leg was thrown over were anything to judge by. The man was a freaking powerhouse. And I was all but laying on top of him.

To make matters worse, the tingle I was feeling low in my belly had nothing to do with being too hot.

"What..." I cleared my throat, struggling to form the correct words. "What are you doing in my bed?"

I felt his body tense beneath mine and went to move, only to have the arm that was holding me in place tighten around me. I realized it was the feel of his fingers sifting through my hair and across my shoulder that was causing the tickling that woke me because he continued the motion once I stopped struggling against the strength of his muscular arm — not because I *wanted* to (or at least that was what I was telling myself), but because it was pointless. He'd always been bigger, but he had at least fifty pounds and four inches on me now, and the struggle was fruitless.

His tone was still gravelly as he asked, "How much of last night do you remember?"

I scanned my memory to try and pick up right where it left off. "Uh... I remember my dad making me come home with you. I remember you helping me to the apartment..." I wracked my brain to try and come up with more, but the pain I'd been experiencing last night seemed to have overshadowed everything that had happened. "Um, maybe an argument you had with Lilly? And... I think I got sick?" I finished, vaguely recalling an up close and personal look at the inside of my toilet bowl.

"You did," he answered in a soft voice. "I thought migraines were rare for you, sweetheart."

I couldn't keep laying there with him, not cuddled up like we were, having what to any outsider would seem like a normal conversation. His arm had loosened so I tried again to escape.

"Ethan, let me up," I said when he refused to let me move off of him for the second time.

"Not until I'm sure you're all right. You scared the shit out of me last night, Eliza."

The burn I'd been feeling earlier was suddenly coming from an angry place, which suited me much better. "Not that it's any of your damn business, but I'm fine," I answered, giving his arm one last hard shove and finally gaining my freedom. Once I was able to put some much needed space between us, I was able to breathe again. Swinging my legs over the side of the bed, I gained my feet and managed to sway only just a bit before righting myself and turning back to see Ethan had sat up, looking way too good on my mattress than was safe for my sanity. "What I want to know is why you thought my condition last night made it okay for you to take advantage. I know you're a fan of shitty behavior, but that was low," I sneered. "Even for you."

I would have liked to claim that I was the bigger person, that I always took the high road, that the way his jaw ticked as he fought to keep his anger at bay didn't make my stomach do a happy little flip, but I wasn't. I'd obviously struck a chord with that last comment, and damn if I wasn't at least the tiniest bit proud of myself.

"Look," he stated with straining patience as he gingerly moved off the bed, grabbing a crutch that I hadn't noticed was leaning against the wall as he made his way toward me. "I know you're pissed—"

"Pissed?" I spat venomously as that anger morphed into a fury so intense it was frightening. "You think that after the awful things you said to me the last time we spoke, I'm only *pissed*?" I didn't miss the way his face twisted with a wince at my reminder of what he'd said to end our friendship, and a loud, uncontrollable bark of sarcastic laughter bubbled up from my throat. I couldn't believe he had the nerve to look contrite. And after six years, no less. My eyes narrowed on him as I continued. "Oh, believe me, Ethan, pissed doesn't even touch the level of anger I have for you."

Despite the hatred I was sure was flashing in my

eyes, he didn't stop his advance until he was only a few inches away from me, his face a mask of regret. "Believe me, I know better than anyone that I deserve every single ounce of hatred you must feel for me. But I'm here to fix that."

I took a step back. "There's no possible way you could fix that, Ethan."

Despite his flinch, he continued to push. "I'm sorry, Eliza," he said in a low, stricken voice. "I'm so fucking sorry."

I took the hit his apology caused and did my best to keep my expression blank. I refused to show him just how much that meant to me. "Too little, six years too late," I spat. With a side-step I attempted to move past him, only to be cut off. He moved surprisingly fast for someone with a torn ACL who depended on a crutch to get around.

Leaning down so we were eye to eye, he repeated, "I'm sorry."

I struggled to hold on to the ire I'd felt since the heartbreak finally faded into the background years ago. "I don't care," I ground out. "I appreciate you helping me home last night. But, as you can see, I'm fine now. You can go."

"I'm sorry!" he stated again, his voice growing louder and fueling my own temper until it finally snapped.

"I don't forgive you!" I stood on my tip toes to yell it in his face. "I'll *never* forgive you!"

"*Don't say that!*" He roared so loud it startled me, causing me to jump backward. My wide-eyed stare took him in cautiously as his chest rose and fell like he'd just finished running a marathon. "Don't... don't fucking say that," he growled, clearly lost in his emotions as he dropped his crutch, clenched his eyes closed, and ran his hands through his hair. He remained in that position, looking utterly consumed by grief, for so long that I was able to notice my own breathing matched the erratic motions of his chest.

"Why do you even care?" I finally asked on a whisper, breaking the charged, palpable silence encompassing the room. "You made it clear what you thought of me with that last phone call." I hated that the emotion clogging my throat could be heard with every word I pushed out. "Then you made it even clearer when you disappeared and *never* came back."

Any space that had been between us disappeared in an instant when he moved on me, cupping my cheeks in both of his warm, calloused palms. It was when his thumb grazed my cheekbone that I realized I had started to cry. The only thing I couldn't stand more than showing my sorrow at losing him was the fact I found myself worried that he was standing there, embracing me, without the support of his crutch.

"That was the biggest mistake I've made in my entire life. I've regretted hurting you every single day, and if you'll let me, I'll do everything in my power to make it up to you. You were my best friend, Eliza. The best friend I've ever had. I'd give my right arm to have that back."

His voice trembled with such reverence it was almost impossible not to believe him. *Almost.* I pulled in a deep breath as I stared straight into his eyes and asked the question that had been plaguing me for the past six years. "Then why'd you do it? You *knew* how everything you said would affect me. It was like you intentionally hit that button my mom created hoping to inflict the most damage. What did I ever do to deserve that?"

"*Nothing.*" His ravaged voice cracked at the same time his fingers on my face twitched, pressing tighter against my skin. "You didn't do anything to deserve it, and I'll hate myself for the rest of my life for what I said to you."

"Then *why?*" I demanded on a shout.

"Because of my own stupid insecurities, sweetheart. You were the most important person in my life, and the closer the draft came, the more I found myself questioning if I really wanted to leave here... to leave you." My eyes widened, still swimming with tears as he continued. "And that scared the shit out of me, Eliza. You knew. You fucking *knew* that all I ever wanted was to get out of here, start my life, to create something that was just mine that I didn't have to worry could be ripped from under me in the blink of an eye. I wanted the security I hadn't had since my grandmother died. But the closer that day got, I started second guessing myself. I knew what your mom did to you and how that fucked with your head and made it hard for you to let people in, and I knew I was fucking *lucky* I was one of those people. I was scared of what would happen to you if I left.

"I actually began considering what my life would be like if I stayed for you so you wouldn't have to feel another loss, and the more I considered it the more fucking terrified I got. I didn't want to give up my dream, and I thought if I didn't make a clean break I was at risk of doing just that, and I worried I'd eventually resent you for it. So I fucked up. I made a huge mistake and I'm. So. Goddamned. Sorry."

I'd always imagined what having Ethan apologize would have felt like, I just never expected it to leave me feeling so... hollow. And in spite of everything he just said, I couldn't shake the sense that he wasn't telling me the full truth. But that was no longer my problem.

Reaching up to wrap my hands around his wrists, I pulled my face free and took a step away, ignoring the hope shining in his golden eyes.

"That's the most selfish, inconsiderate thing I've ever heard in my life," I managed to grind out. The tears immediately dried up, leaving me feeling cold and empty. "See, the difference between me and you is that I would never, *ever* have let you give up what you loved for me. I would have missed you... of course I would have, you were my best friend. But I was *happy* for you. Fucking thrilled! I would have never asked or expected you to give up your dream for me."

"Eliza—"

I smacked his hand away when he reached for me again. "Everything you put me through, everything you said... it was all because you were a coward," I spat, my lip curling in disgust. "I would have been happy with phone calls and texts, with getting to watch every goddamned game you played and telling everyone 'Hey look! That's my best friend.' I would have been happy because I had my *best friend*. But because you were weak, you took that away from me in the most painful way you could think of. And now you come back and expect me to actually forgive you?"

I let out a bewildered laugh as I looked up at the ceiling, as if asking for divine assistance before meeting his crushed gaze once more. "I'll be civil. When we're forced to be in the same room because of our families, I'll put on a happy face and play nice. And when you leave, I'll go back to living my life the same way I've been since you *purposely* disappeared from it. But don't ask me for anything else. I'm not the little, insecure girl I was when you left. I know what I'm worth now. I know what I deserve, and it's more than the bullshit you gave me." Once I finished my tirade, my chest swelled with pride that I hadn't caved, that I stood my ground and demanded more for myself. "Now, if you'll be so kind as to let yourself out, I've got a life to live. And you're no longer a part of that."

When I moved around him that time he didn't stop me. I'd just made it to my bedroom door and pulled it open, fully intending on leaving him without so much as a backward glance when his voice, suddenly so full of determination, stopped me on the spot.

"Eliza." I didn't turn. But I did look back at him over my shoulder, only to feel a tremor shoot up my spine at the smile that graced his gorgeous face. "I'm glad to know you're not that little girl anymore. And just so you know, I've changed too." I opened my mouth to ask, spitefully, if he wanted a pat on the back, but he wasn't finished. "And a word of warning, before I leave this town, I *will* get my best friend back. Even if I have to bend over backward and break every fucking bone in my body to do it. I'll get your trust again. No matter fucking what."

Suddenly peeved that I hadn't ended our conversation with the upper hand, I threw the door the rest of the way open and stomped into the bathroom across the hallway, slamming that door behind me. All the while, telling myself that the low sound of his chuckle didn't make my insides feel all tingly...

Even though it really did.

Chapter Thirteen

Ethan

THERE WAS A strong possibility that I was pushing my luck, but I had reached the point where I no longer gave a fuck. It had been two weeks since the blow up with Eliza in her bedroom, and every day since then, I'd come up with some excuse to be in her presence. Yes, I was aware that what I was doing could have been considered stalking to some, but I preferred to think of it as being fiercely determined. On the plus side, because of my "determination," I'd gotten to eat at least one meal a day at the café, and damn, that girl could cook her ass off.

But I knew my constant attention was starting to wear on Eliza when, not even an hour ago, she came storming out of the kitchen demanding to know if I intended to "bug the shit out of her" for the remainder of my time in Pembrooke at a volume loud enough for everyone in the café to hear.

Needless to say, she didn't find me endearing when I announced—just as loudly—that I planned on "bugging the shit out of her" for as long as it took to get her to forgive me and give me my friend back. She let out an adorable huff, followed by a myriad of curses that seemed out of character for her, before storming back into the kitchen.

That was why I currently found myself sitting at one of the comfortable booths that made up Sinful Sweets Café eating my third—or was it my fourth?—bowl of white bean chili when a blast from my past slid into the seat across from me, stating in a voice laced with humor, "Well look who's decided to grace our town with his presence."

My head came up from where it had been hovering over my bowl as I shoveled food in. "Holy shit," I muttered, a grin spreading across my face at the sight of the man sitting in front of me. "Quinn fucking Mallick." The guy I'd spent three years playing high school football with smiled in return and reached across the table to shake my extended hand. "How the hell have you been, man? I'm surprised to see you back here. Didn't you move away shortly after graduation? Seattle or something like that?"

"Yeah." He shrugged casually and leaned back and rested his arms against the back of the booth. "Life changes, man. What can I say? Moved back here when my little girl was four. Remembered what it was like growing up here and wanted to give her that same thing."

"Wow, man. You've got a little girl? That's awesome."

Pride shone in Quinn's expression as he shifted to pull his cell from his back pocket. He hit a couple buttons on the screen before sliding it across the table. Staring back from the screen was a little blonde-haired, blue-eyed girl with a huge smile on her face, complete with missing front teeth and everything. "She's a cutie," I told him, handing the phone back. "You're gonna have a problem on your hands when she gets old enough to date."

He made a noise in the back of his throat that indicated he already knew that. "Believe me, she's only in kindergarten this year, and I'm already dreading her teenage years. And she'll *never* be old enough to date if I have a say in it."

With a chuckle, I stated, "Well she's definitely got her mom's good looks. If she was as ugly as you, you'd never have to worry about the boys beating her door down."

Quinn's smile seemed a little darker as he looked back at the photo on his phone before shutting it down and sliding it back into his pocket. "Yeah, she's her mom's girl, that's for damn sure." I wasn't sure what was going on in his head, but whatever it was, the look on his face made it clear not to push. I opened my mouth to move us to a new topic when Eliza's presence hit me before she'd even made it to the table. With all the delicious smells floating around the restaurant, I could still make out her almond and vanilla scent from feet away.

She stopped at the edge, set two large plastic bags full of Styrofoam containers on the table, and sent Quinn a friendly smile, all the while pretending I wasn't even there. "Hey, Quinn. I got your order. Hope you haven't been waiting too long."

At the sight of her happy, smiling face pointed in the direction of my one-time friend, a completely irrational sense of jealousy washed over me.

"Nah," Quinn grinned back, standing from his side of the booth and stepping out, "had just enough time to catch up with this asshole before having to get back to the station." He threw his thumb in my direction, and it wasn't lost on me that Eliza's head didn't turn my way.

"Well, stay safe," Eliza frowned playfully, setting my teeth on edge.

"Safe?" I questioned, inserting myself in their conversation since they hadn't been polite enough to include me.

"Yeah." Quinn pointed to the Pembrooke Fire Department insignia on the right side of his jacket that I hadn't noticed until just then. "Working over at Station Two. Just stopped in to pick up lunch for me and the guys." He leaned in for another handshake, which I returned, while stating, "Good catching up, man. If you're back for a while, we should go out for beers or something. It's been too long."

"Yeah, we'll do that," I replied. With a tilt of his chin my way, and a kiss to Eliza's cheek, Quinn headed out the door. Eliza turned to retreat, but I grabbed hold of her wrist before she could escape.

"You know he's married with a kid, right?" I said on a low growl. "You really think you should be flirting with him?"

With a sharp yank, she pulled her wrist from my grasp, but instead of leaving, she leaned in, speaking in a furious hiss only loud enough for me to hear. "That wasn't flirting, asshole. That was me being nice to someone who's always been nice to me. It's called common courtesy. Maybe you should try it some time."

"Eliza—"

"And for the record, his wife passed away. But you'd know that if your inconsiderate ass came home or followed up with your friends every once in a while."

Shit. Just when I thought I couldn't have felt more like an asshole in the weeks I'd been back in Pembrooke, I stuck my foot in my mouth and did something to prove there were even more layers to my asshole-ness than I originally thought.

"If you're done with your meal, please feel free to pay your tab, tip the waitress, and leave." Her tone might have sounded polite, but the way she said it meant it wasn't so much a suggestion as a demand.

"Shit, Eliza. I'm sorry," I breathed, running a hand through my hair.

"You know, you've been saying that a lot lately."

"Because I mean it!" I bit back.

"Then stop saying it and start showing it, Ethan. What have you actually *done* to prove to me or anybody in this town that you're sorry for being a shitty friend or a shitty brother for the past six years?"

Jesus Christ, she hadn't been kidding when she said she'd changed. The Eliza I knew was always headstrong, but she'd never been one to make a scene or give someone a verbal ass kicking, even when they deserved it. Clearly, with age came a sharp tongue where Eliza

Anderson was concerned. And fuck if it wasn't sexy as hell to see her reacting with so much passion.

Before I had a chance to apologize again, or maybe do something stupid like tell her just how gorgeous I found her in that very moment. Another presence interrupted our standoff. And, unlike Quinn's appearance, that particular blast from the past was unwanted, and very unwelcome.

"Hi, Ethan. I thought that was you."

Even if the feminine voice wasn't familiar to me—in that nails-on-a-chalkboard kind of way—the way Eliza's entire body went rigid and her face blanked would have told me exactly who was standing behind her.

I knew good and well that Eliza couldn't stand my on-again-off-again ex-girlfriend Shannon, and she had every right. I'd started dating her my freshman year of high school. She was a year ahead of me in school, sixteen years old, and more than willing to put out with any of the guys from the varsity football team. And seeing as I was a dumbass kid who was only thinking with his dick, I thought she'd walked on water, and throughout the next four years, we broke up and got back together more times than I could count on either hand. She cheated, had a nasty jealous streak, was a spoiled, entitled little brat, and my sister never liked her. Those red flags should have been enough for me to realize that not only wasn't she a good girlfriend, but she pretty much sucked as a human being all together.

Over the years, one of Shannon's hot buttons was my relationship with Eliza. Because she didn't understand what our friendship was like back then, and she felt that she was the only person without a dick I should have been allowed to talk to, she took a distinct dislike to Eliza. And let it show.

She treated Eliza like shit whenever she thought I wouldn't find out about it, bullying her and being as cruel and nasty as a bitch like her could possibly be, thinking her pussy was enough to keep me on a leash while she secretly treated my best friend like shit. We fought about it constantly, because if I wasn't there to see it myself, someone else always managed to tell me what evil Shannon was up to when I wasn't around. Because Eliza was so young and quiet, she most certainly wouldn't have told me herself.

It wasn't until I pulled my head out of my ass and finally noticed just how closed off Eliza became whenever Shannon was around that I finally pulled the cord, ending things for good.

But Shannon, being the worst kind of bitch, didn't use our breakup as a reason to stop her torment of Eliza. She'd never been one to apply herself to much of anything, so while I was in college, she was still in

Pembrooke, trying to hold on to her old glory days from high school. I could remember multiple occasions where I'd have to drive my ass all the way from Laramie just so I could hold Eliza while she cried after Shannon had done something particularly mean. I hated not being in the same town to stop my jealous ex, but Eliza swore up and down she didn't need my protection.

That didn't stop me from hauling my ass over to Shannon's house on multiple occasions and ripping the woman a new asshole. Unfortunately it never helped.

Suddenly discovering that venomous woman was still living in the same town as my sweet, mild-mannered (or at least she used to be) best friend made every muscle in my body lock, ready to battle.

"Shannon," I spoke through clenched teeth, refusing to take my eyes off Eliza as the other woman bumped against her shoulder in an effort to get closer to me.

"I heard you were back," she said in a low voice that I was sure men who didn't realize what a blood-sucking shrew she was would find seductive. I wasn't one of them. Reaching across the table, she ran a painted nail along the back of my hands as she continued with that ridiculous fucking voice. "It's been a long time. I was hoping we could catch up."

"Hasn't been long enough, and as far as I'm concerned there's nothing to catch up on. I'm just here, catching up with an old friend and trying to enjoy my meal. So..." Anyone else would have taken the hint and taken off before they did something to embarrass themselves. But not her. Because heartless skanks had no shame.

"Well I'll join you," she said cheerfully, shoving Eliza out of the way in order to claim the bench across from me.

My mouth opened to object, but my girl got there first, shocking the hell out of me while filling my chest with pride all at the same time. "Sorry, but I'm going to have to ask you to leave," she said in a syrupy sweet voice.

Shannon looked at her with a hateful glare. "What? Why?"

"There's a sign clearly posted outside that states 'no shoes, no shirt, no service' and seeing as half your shirt looks like it was ripped off by a mountain lion or something before you walked in here, your clothing choices aren't meeting the standards of this particular establishment." And just to add insult to injury, she added, sweetly, "Maybe try the Denny's on the other side of town? I just hope their *no dogs allowed* policy won't count for you."

"Who the hell do you think you are, you stupid, frumpy bitch?!" Shannon started to stand, but I shot from my seat and stood in front of Eliza faster. After that display I had no doubt she could do more than just hold her own, but she'd said her piece. If Shannon was stupid enough not to get that she wasn't wanted, I was going to clear things up. There was no reason for Eliza to be forced to engage any further than she already had.

"No one invited you to sit here," I told her, the tone of my voice causing her eyes to grow wide.

"But... Ethan—"

I cut her off, not feeling bad in the slightest. "I didn't ask you to join me for lunch, and I sure as fuck don't want you sitting across from me while I'm trying to keep my food down. So since Eliza doesn't want you here, and *I* sure as shit don't want you here, there's no reason for you to stay."

"Babe, just let me—"

"We have nothing to catch up on seeing as the last words I ever spoke to you were that if I ever found out you so much as *looked* at Eliza wrong, I'd make your life miserable. You clearly didn't listen, so it looks like I'll have to make good on my promise."

I could hear the muffled voices and movement from the people straining to hear, but other than Shannon's spiteful words, they hadn't been able to hear the full exchange, which did nothing but make her look like an even bigger fool since most of the town had always thought Eliza to be the sweetest.

"You're still standing here," a sarcastic voice spoke up from behind me. I barely suppressed an eye roll when I turned to look over my shoulder to give Eliza a *really? Could you not right now* look.

She shrugged, but had the grace to look properly scolded.

It was the pure hate in Shannon's voice that forced my head to turn back around as she spoke, "You always chose her over me." She spit as her eyes shot fire in my direction. "That twisted, weird little relationship you guys had back then was creepy and it's still fucking creepy today."

I shrugged. "Rather be in a relationship only *you* would consider creepy than stuck with a heartless bitch like you."

She moved to slap me, a motion I would have had no problem blocking had a particular little ball of fire not jumped in front of me and grabbed Shannon's wrist before I could. "You slap him and, so help me God, I'll rip your hair out at the roots. Now get the hell out of *my* building before I have someone call the cops and escort your ass out."

We both watched in silence as a red-faced, clearly

embarrassed Shannon spun on her hooker heels and stomped out of the café.

"Well..." I breathed, gaining Eliza's attention. "That was fun."

She rolled her eyes and shook her head as she turned and headed back for the kitchen, but not before I saw the corners of her mouth twitching with a suppressed smile.

Progress.

Chapter Fourteen

Eliza

"So what do you think? I'm wondering if the choreography's going to be too hard for my intermediate class."

Lilly's voice jerked me out of my distracting thoughts. "Sorry. What?"

With a sigh and eye roll, she moved over to where her iPod was docked and turned it off just as another song started to play before coming to sit next to me on the floor where my back was resting against the wall. "If you're not going to pay attention, you might as well not even be here," she grumbled, but I knew her well enough to know she wasn't really mad, just perturbed at my lack of attention.

"I don't even know why you ask me to come down here and watch your routines. I don't know the first thing about dancing. How could I possibly be any help to you?" I asked, watching our reflection in the mirrored wall across from us as I nudged her shoulder with my own.

She nudged back. "That's the point. Most of the people in the audience during the Winter Showcase don't know the first thing about dance," she answered, talking about the recital her students put on every holiday season for the entire town. "All they know is that they enjoy watching it. That's what you're here for, to tell me what you're watching is pretty so I know the rest of the town will like it."

I smiled at her through the mirror even though she was sitting right next to me. "So all I'm here for is to tell you that you're pretty?"

"Exactly!"

We both burst into laughter. Once we'd gotten that under control, Lilly spoke up. "So I heard there was a kerfuffle at the café the other day."

"Seriously?" I chuckled. "Who says *kerfuffle*?"

She gave me a tiny shrug. "Not enough people, if you ask me. It's a great word."

I gave that some thought. "It actually is. We should try and bring it back."

"On it. Now stop trying to change the subject. What happened at the café?"

I sighed, hating just how well Lilly knew me. "It wasn't a big deal, really," I fibbed, trying to downplay the entire thing. "Shannon showed up."

"God, I can't stand that woman," Lilly seethed, voicing exactly what I was thinking. "She never goes in there. She knows that's your domain. Why on earth would she start coming in now?"

I turned my head and gave her a *don't-ask-stupid-questions* look. "Why do you think? Ethan was in there. She must think she still has some sort of claim on his dick or something."

"Brilliant," she gritted sarcastically. "It's like high school for you all over again."

I thought of what Ethan had said to Shannon about the last time they talked. "Ethan said something interesting during that whole scene. Apparently, the last time him and Shannon talked, he threatened her about messing with me."

Lilly's eyes got big. "No way. You believe him?"

"Well," I thought about it. "It would make sense. After he went off to college, she turned into an even bigger bitch than before, doing her best to make my life a living Hell. I never told him about it, but one day it all just... stopped. She'd give me dirty looks whenever I'd see her, but all the childish bullshit stopped. I thought she'd just gotten tired of picking on someone who refused to engage."

"And now you think Ethan had something to do with it?"

"You should have seen her face," I admitted, somewhat gleefully. "As soon as he said he was going to make good on his threat, she freaked. Then she got pissed. She even tried to slap him."

"Damn it!" Lilly's sharp words echoed loudly through the open space. "I always miss the good stuff!"

"Poor Lilly," I teased. "I'll make sure to call you beforehand next time there's drama."

She grinned big. "Much appreciated." As we sat in silence in the empty studio, I began to hope that she'd drop the subject of Ethan. I should have known better. Lilly was nothing if not persistent.

"So, he stood up for you in front of an entire restaurant full of people, almost earning himself a bitch slap in the process."

I shot her a side-eyed look. "What's your point?"

"No point," she said a little too casually. "Just wondering if this means you've forgiven him. First stalking, now going head to head with evil exes that threaten you... I have to say, the boy's been pretty busy lately."

"Lilly—" I started, warningly, a sense of growing agitation coming over me as she gave life to exactly what

I'd been feeling ever since Ethan's return. I naively believed that if I could just ignore everything I was feeling in regards to him, if I could just wait him out until he eventually left, that I'd be fine, but the longer he persisted the harder it was for me to keep faith that my life would eventually go back to what it had been before he re-entered the picture and disrupted everything. For all these reasons, I'd been avoiding any discussion of Ethan with Lilly. And it seemed like she'd finally had enough.

"Don't you '*Lilly*' me, like you really think that tone of voice scares me at all."

"Look, I really don't want to talk about this right now, okay? I just want..." I trailed off, suddenly not sure what it *was* I actually wanted.

"To keep your head buried in the sand until he leaves again, so you can act like nothing's changed," she finished for me.

"Yes. That. Exactly that. And if you were a true friend, you'd help me dig that hole then go about your business."

Her chest puffed out with something akin to pride. "Lucky for you, I'm an exceptionally shitty friend."

"Yay. So lucky," I grumbled flatly.

She clapped her hands and rubbed them together gleefully. "Now, let's go home, crack open a bottle of wine or three, get completely annihilated, and you can tell me all about how you're eventually going to cave when it comes to the yummy Ethan Prewitt."

I looked over at my best friend, trying my hardest not to smile. "I hate you. But you have wine, so I'm willing to overlook your short comings for the time being."

"Big of you," she chuckled as she stood and reached for my hand to help me off the floor. "Now let's go get shitfaced."

That was the best plan I'd heard in days.

I ABSOLUTELY LOVED FALL IN PEMBROOKE. LIVING in a valley surrounded by mountains covered in trees as the leaves turned different shades of red, orange, and yellow was the kind of beauty most other places lacked. The chill in the air was enough to make you grab for a light jacket and scarf, but not enough to bite at your skin when you went outside. But my favorite thing about fall was the smell of wood smoke that seemed to fill the air as people in town began lighting fires in their fireplaces. Fall gave you that giddy, excited feeling that winter was just around the corner, and while most people viewed Thanksgiving as the start of the holiday season, for me, it all began with Halloween.

"Thank you so much for helping," Harlow panted as she dropped the box of decorations on the linoleum floor.

"I help every year," I laughed. "Eventually you have to stop thanking me and just accept that it's a given."

"Oh, shut up and help me get these spider webs set up before the game starts," she said with a grin. It was Friday evening and just like I'd done for the past several years, Chloe, Lilly, and I were helping Harlow set up the high school gymnasium for the Halloween dance which would take place once the football game ended. It was tradition in our town for everyone to attend the game just before Halloween in costume, and even though I wasn't a huge fan of the sport—anymore at least—I still loved coming to this particular game. Truth be told, it was one of the only games I attended each year since Ethan graduated high school. With people like Shannon in the stands, my love for football had started to lose some of its luster. Then everything with Ethan happened and... well, it stopped holding any appeal at all.

"Did you bring your costume to change into?" Chloe asked, pulling me out of my head.

I stepped up onto the ladder and taped the spider webs in place. "Yep," I answered as I climbed back down to move the ladder a few feet and repeat the process.

"What are you going to be this year?" Harlow asked.

I twisted my neck from where I stood at the top of the ladder and looked at the three woman staring up at me. "A witch," I answered simply. "Same as every year."

"How creative," Lilly mumbled, earning laughs from Chloe and Harlow.

"There's nothing wrong with my costume," I defended. "It's perfectly fine."

"It's boring!" Lilly countered. "You don't even technically dress up. You just put on a hat and fake nose. You can do better than that."

"Well you'll just have to deal with it. We're almost done here, and it's the only costume I have." The calculating smile that spread across all three of their faces made me nervous. "Wait... What did you do?"

"Nothing," Chloe chirped playfully. "Just went out and got a new costume for you to wear this year." She practically skipped over to the duffle bag sitting on one of the decked out tables. She unzipped the bag and pulled out a costume that was missing at least half of its fabric.

"No," I declared, climbing off the ladder and planting my hands on my hips. "No way in hell. This is a school function, Chloe! What the hell are you thinking? I can't go as a slutty cheerleader to a high school football game!"

"Oh, get your grannie panties out of a twist, you prude," Lilly said with an exaggerated roll of her eyes. "It's not slutty. You're just being a baby about it."

I crossed my arms over my chest and scowled. "Am not."

"Are too."

"Not!"

"Too!"

"Oh, for the love of God," Harlow sighed. "I feel like I'm watching Lucy and Evan fight."

"She started it!" I pouted. "And I'm not wearing that."

"You are," Lilly argued.

"I'm not!"

"Are!"

"Enough!" When Chloe used her Mom voice, there was no choice but to listen. "You're wearing this because you're twenty-two years old and have a fabulous body. It's not slutty, and that witch costume is played out. Besides, you don't have any other choice. Lilly already went through your bag and threw that stupid hat and nose away."

With an outraged gasp, my eyes bounced to each woman, all of them wearing shit-eating grins. "You guys suck so bad," I exclaimed on an exhale, knowing full well

I had no choice but to wear the stupid, clichéd cheer-leader costume.

"You love us," Harlow announced, taking the costume from Chloe and slapping it against my chest. "Now go get changed. The game's about to start."

"What about you guys?" I asked.

"Please," Chloe scoffed. "Harlow and I are too old for costumes."

"And I have to get back to the studio to work on a number for the showcase so I won't be at the game," Lilly answered.

With a few more grumbles and some not-so-nice name calling, I slumped my shoulders and headed for the nearest girls' bathroom, all the while cursing my life and the pushy as hell people I'd let into it.

Chapter Fifteen

Ethan

I WAS JUST reaching for the doors to the gym when they pushed open and Lilly came prancing through. "Wow," she laughed, taking in my get up. "Original."

I looked down at my old high school football jersey that I'd managed to scrounge up in one of the closets at Harlow's. It was tighter on my chest and arms than it had been back in the day, but other than that, it fit. That, a pair of jeans and eye black slashed under my eyes was the extent of my costume. "Hey, you try coming up with a decent costume when you have to wear this goddamned brace with everything."

Her grin was lacking any of the animosity she had been holding over me the past few weeks. "Well, it's actually fitting if you think about it," she mumbled more to herself than me.

Choosing to ignore her bizarre statement, I asked, "Harlow and Chloe inside? Their husbands sent me on a search and rescue mission."

"Yep, just finishing up. Go on in."

I watched as she started for the parking lot. "You're not staying for the game?"

"Not my sport," she called out, turning to walk backward. "I prefer hockey. You know, a game that requires *real* skill."

I placed my hand over my heart, faking pain as she threw her head back and laughed before spinning around and tossing a wave over her shoulder. "Enjoy your night, Football Star."

"I really wish people'd stop calling me that!" I shouted back.

"It's either that, or World's Dumbest Asshole. I figured I'd go with the nicer this time around." With that, she climbed into her car and shut the door. Seconds later it started up and she took off. I wasn't sure what I'd done to get off her shit list, but whatever it was, I'd take it, seeing as it seemed she and Eliza were a package deal.

Walking into the decked out gym was like stepping into a time machine. Even though it looked like

Halloween had thrown up all over the place, I felt like I'd been transported into the past, a past with some not-so-great memories, but a whole hell of a lot of good ones. I was quickly discovering that the longer I stayed in Pembrooke, the more I came to realize the good had far outweighed the bad. Then again, you know what they say about hindsight.

As I walked further in, my eyes finally landed on my sister and her friend Chloe. "Hey ladies," I spoke up, stepping next to Harlow and planting a kiss on her cheek before giving Chloe the same gesture. "Noah and Derrick sent me in to look for you. Told me to tell you two to move your asses, but seeing as I'm a gentleman, I'll leave that last part out."

Harlow rolled her eyes before smacking me in the chest and moved to throw away the empty wrapping the Halloween decorations came in. "All these years and that man still doesn't have any damn patience."

Chloe's laugh had me turning her way just in time to see something gleaming in her eyes before she managed to mask it. "We're heading out now. Eliza's in the bathroom, changing into her costume. You mind waiting for her?"

My chest tightened as my heart rate picked up at the mention of Eliza's name. "Sure," I answered a little too quickly, earning weird glances from both women. But I was still struggling with my newfound feelings for Eliza as it was, I didn't have time to try and decipher every strange look I got from the people in my life.

I'd meant it when I told Eliza I wanted my best friend back, and I was determined to get that, but the more I got to know her, different nuances of her personality that hadn't been there before rose to the surface. Or maybe they'd always been there, it was just that she hadn't discovered them by the time I disappeared on her. Either way, I was growing to like what I saw with each passing day, which made looking at her as just a friend increasingly difficult.

As if I didn't have enough on my plate already just trying to earn her trust back. If she knew the thoughts that ran through my head when it came to her, she'd probably never say another fucking word to me.

"You guys should get going before Noah sends an announcement over the PA system."

Harlow grabbed an empty box from one of the tables as they both moved for the door. Chloe turned to look at me before they walked out "Hurry her up, would you? She tends to drag her feet when she's not happy about something."

My brows drew together. "What's she not happy about?"

Chloe grinned as Harlow laughed. "You'll see."

The gym door shut with a resounding clang, leaving me alone in what looked like the setting from *A Nightmare Before Christmas.*

I kept checking my watch, waiting for Eliza to come out of the bathroom so I could take her back to the football field, but five minutes had passed and the door to the restroom still hadn't opened.

Worry began creeping in. What if she's fallen and hit her head or something? What if the lock on the door was faulty and she was trapped inside. Shit like that happened in older buildings all the time... or so I told myself.

I gave her another two minutes before I made my way over to the door and gave it a firm knock before pushing it open and poking my head through.

"Eliza?"

"Ethan?" Her tone was sharp with surprise. I stepped fully into the bathroom, my sight still blocked by the small wall that cut off the doorway to the rest of the bathroom. "What are you doing in here?"

"Chloe and Harlow headed to the field. I told them I'd wait for you. Got worried it was taking a while. You okay?"

"Uh..." her voice trailed off, causing me to take a step

passed the wall only to find the area in front of the sinks empty.

"Where are you?"

There was a long pause, then, "In the first stall."

I looked down and, sure enough, there were her feet in a pair of god-awful white shoes and little socks with pompoms on the backs. "What's wrong?"

"Well... my zipper's kind of stuck."

The tension in my shoulders drained away. "Come out. Let me help you."

"No."

My chuckle bounced off the tile walls all around us. "Eliza, come on. Just let me help. What are you going to do? Stay in here all night?"

"No. I fully intend on waiting you out, then changing back into my other clothes."

I looked around the space and spotted a gray and teal bag sitting on one of the sinks I hadn't noticed before. Walking over to it, I discovered it held Eliza's clothes. "You mean the clothes in this bag out here?"

"Yes," she answered hesitantly, cautiously. It might have been years, and we might both be different, but she still knew me, whether she'd admit it or not, and her trepidation was completely warranted.

"You mean the bag I'm holding in my hand right

now?" I asked, pulling the straps of her bag over my shoulder.

"Ethan," she said in a warning voice as her hand popped out from under the stall door. "Give me my bag right now."

A big grin spread across my lips. "Can't do that, sweetheart. We're already running late. Now get your cute ass out here and let me help you with that zipper."

"I hate you."

"And I'm working to change that. Now open the door. Stop being so damned stubborn."

"You're one to talk!" she shouted back with a clipped, bewildered laugh. "You're practically stalking me, and *you're* calling *me* stubborn?"

"I wouldn't have to stalk you if you'd forgive me and be my friend again." *And maybe something more*, I thought but managed to bite my tongue to keep from saying out loud. I had enough work on my hands already.

Her sigh carried from the stall. She remained silent for several seconds before finally speaking again, this time much more quietly, her words flaying me wide open. "I wouldn't have to forgive you if you hadn't hurt me."

"Baby," I choked, moving toward the stall door and

resting my forehead against it. "I'm so sorry. If there was a way to take it all back, I would. I swear."

She didn't say anything, only sniffled, and the thought that she could possibly be crying was a shot to the chest. "Please open the door, sweetheart. I'm not leaving until you do."

A few seconds—that felt like a lifetime—later, the lock clicked and the door swung open, and what I saw standing before me, stunned me speechless. "Fine, you win," she huffed and she propped her hands on her hips in a belligerent stance. Thankfully her eyes were devoid of any tears. "Help me zip this damn thing so we can go."

"Holy fuck," I wheezed, my mouth hanging open as my eyes scanned the sheer decadence standing in front of me. "Holy *fuck*."

"What? What's wrong with it?" she asked, fidgeting from foot to foot as she tried in vain to pull the short cheerleader skirt down to a modest length. Seeing all that was Eliza, all those womanly curves and gorgeous legs dressed up as a cheerleader was the most intoxicating torture. All the blood in my head rushed straight to my dick, and I had to drop the duffle bag on my arm in order to hide it.

"Do I look okay?" she asked, suddenly sounding uncertain, like she had absolutely no idea just how beautiful she was. Which only made her that much more alluring. But seeing her like that had fried my brain. I couldn't think, let alone form words. A garbled noise came out of my throat.

"I knew it!" she cried at the strange sound I'd just made. "I look ridiculous! This is all Chloe and Harlow's fault! I can't wear this."

"What in the fresh hell were they thinking?!" I shouted, startling her out of her own tantrum. "You can't wear that! It's... it's... *Christ*! It's completely indecent!"

No one but me should have been allowed to see her like that... not that I'd ever say that out loud, well, at least not until we were on more solid footing.

Suddenly the unease melted from her expression, replaced with a menacing glare... aimed right at me. "Oh my God! You're doing it again!"

"Doing what?"

Her index finger shot out, jabbing right against my breast bone. "Being an overprotective jerk!"

"If trying to keep you from getting arrested for indecent exposure is being an overprotective jerk, then so fucking be it."

Her head tipped back in a laugh of disbelief. "You've always done this! You were always acting like my pain-in-the-ass big brother, telling me I couldn't wear certain things, go out with certain people—"

I cut her off, feeling the intense need to defend myself. "I only did that twice. And that was because those shorts actually showed ass cheek! You should have been thanking me. If Derrick had seen that, he'd have killed you then had an aneurism. You're welcome. And as for telling you who you could see, you know as well as I do that Jason McKinney was a tool. If I had let you go out with him that night, you'd have been arrested right along with him. Again... you're welcome."

Her mouth opened and closed repeatedly as she attempted (and failed) to come up with a solid argument. She knew I was right.

"Well... whatever."

"You're not wearing that," I commanded. If I'd have been in my right mind, I would have seen that I'd just made my first mistake.

"Like hell I'm not! You can't treat me like your little sister. I'm a grown woman and can do whatever the hell I want!"

Oh, if only she knew my actions had absolutely nothing to do with viewing her as a little sister, and *everything* to do with insane jealousy at just the thought of another man seeing her like that.

"Now zip me up, and let's go."

"No," I answered authoritatively, crossing my arms over my chest. That was my second mistake.

"No?" she asked in a frighteningly low voice.

"That's right. No. You can't go out there in that. You'll... catch pneumonia." *Oh, for fuck's sake.* Third and final mistake.

"Ethan Prewitt," she growled, taking a step close to me, her face twisted into a scowl so scary I was forced to take a step back. "You zip this skirt up right now, or so help me God, I'll walk out of this gym with it hanging wide open for all of Pembrooke to see. And don't for one second think I won't do it. Remember what happened last time you called my bluff?"

My mind scanned back to when she was sixteen years old. I'd been home from college one weekend and Eliza had asked me to take her to a party some of the kids were having out by the lake. Being the responsible adult I was, and not wanting her to get shit-faced and possibly drown that night, I'd refused. She threw a typical teenage tantrum, going on about having to grow up too soon and how she wanted to just be a normal teenager for one night. I didn't cave, even when she threatened to steal her dad's keys and drive there herself.

I called that particular bluff, never once thinking she'd actually do it, seeing as her dad was a cop *and* she was such a horrible driver she'd failed Driver's Ed once already. I'd been very, *very* wrong. That night ended with Derrick's truck in a ditch as he shouted until he was red in the face while Chloe and I stood along the shoulder, watching the tow truck driver pull the truck out of mud up to the top of the wheel wells. Only plus side to that night was the fact that she'd run off the road *before* making it to that party. God only knew how much worse it could have been had alcohol been involved.

So I knew she'd do it, just to spite me. If I'd have just kept my fucking mouth shut, she probably would have changed back into her regular clothes and we'd have never had to have the conversation in the first goddamned place. Me and my big fucking mouth.

"Turn around," I ground out, the muscle in my jaw ticking.

She did just that, but not before gracing me with a triumphant, incredibly smug grin. But that wasn't what made every muscle in my body lock up. Oh no, that was all thanks to the pale pink, lacy thong that showed through the opening of the zipper.

As if my erection wasn't already bad enough, at the minuscule sight of that lace and that tanned, soft looking flesh, my cock actually began to twitch. Sliding the duffle up my arm to free my hand, I gave the zipper a couple of firm tugs, finally unsticking it and getting the skirt closed. But the image was already burned into my brain.

"Thank you," she said in a chipper voice now that

she'd gotten her way. "Let's go. They're probably wondering what's taking us so long."

With that, she waltzed from the bathroom, leaving me to follow as I clutched her bag in front of my pants, praying my hard on would disappear before I came face to face with her father.

Fuck my life.

Chapter Sixteen

Eliza

SHIT.

I was cold. Not that I'd ever admit it out loud, but I could at least admit to myself that I might not have given much thought to the temperature outside when I stormed out of the gym in an effort to stick it to Ethan.

I had the oddest sensation of feeling his eyes on me as he walked a few steps behind all the way to the stadium and up the bleachers. To my bewilderment, he even took my hand as we made our ascent. When I cast a questioning look over my shoulder, he simply shrugged and muttered something about wanting to be able to catch me if I tripped.

That, coupled with the chill in the air, caused a

tremor to course through me as we moved through the crowd of people to our seats that were being held by both of our families. Ethan, being who he was — the hometown superstar — was stopped constantly to say hello to people he'd known growing up, or to sign the random autograph. I did my best to keep moving every time he was stopped, but the fingers wrapped around mine would tighten, making it impossible to escape. He signed everything one handed, refusing to release my hand until we made it to our spots.

"What the hell are you wearing?" My father demanded once we hit our destination. "Jesus, baby girl. Are you *trying* to give me a heart attack?"

I rolled my eyes, along with Harlow and Chloe as Ethan muttered, "Told you," from behind me, earning an elbow to the ribs. The big brother act had gotten old when we were younger, but having him slide back into that role now that we were in adulthood was even more irritating.

"I think she looks pretty!" Abbi declared from the bleachers directly in front of us where she sat with Cate, Lucy, and Evan. It was safe to say I *loved* my little sister at that very moment.

"Thank you, honey," I smiled.

"She looks naked is what she looks like," Dad grumbled just before Chloe reached up and smacked him in the back of the head. "What?" he asked, looking at her, trying his best to appear innocent. "Can't a father worry about his daughter's wellbeing? I mean she's liable to catch pneumonia wearing that ridiculous costume."

Ethan leaned around me to tell my father, "That's exactly what I said."

I put my palm to his face and shoved him back before turning back to my dad. "There's absolutely nothing wrong with my costume," I snapped, my hands on my hips as I shot lasers his way.

"It's short," he replied.

"It's fine," I gritted back.

"I can see too much of your legs."

"I wanna be a cheerleader next year!" Cate shouted.

"Over my dead fucking body," Dad responded, giving Chloe no choice but to hit him in the back of the head again.

"Derrick! Language!"

Knowing there was no way he'd win, not with Chloe and Harlow on my side, he grumbled unintelligible words under his breath and turned his gaze back toward the field, pouting the entire time.

I moved to take my seat on the cold metal bleacher between Harlow and Ethan when someone called my name.

"Eliza?"

My head turned to the left and I smiled when I spotted the person who'd just called out. "Hey Kevin."

Kevin Vincent had been in my grade all through school. We'd never really been friends, more like casual acquaintances since he was always chronically awkward and shy growing up. He went off to college after graduating and had only recently come back. I remembered thinking that becoming an adult had worked a miracle for him. Gone was the shy teenager that I'd known for years, and in his place was an extremely attractive man. One of the things that made Kevin even more attractive to all the women in Pembrooke was the fact that he hadn't shed the mentality that he'd had all his life. So on top of his good looks, he was very humble and sensitive.

And that worked wonders for him from what I'd heard through the Pembrooke grapevine.

"Wow," he returned my grin, a hank of his brown hair falling forward across his forehead, "I love your costume. You look great."

I chose to ignore my dad when I heard him mutter, "Should have brought my goddamned gun," under his breath.

"Thank you." I looked at Ethan to find him glaring daggers in Kevin's direction. "Scoot down," I told him, pulling his attention to me where I was still standing.

"What? Why?"

"So I can talk to Kevin without having to lean over you."

His brow furrowed with an intense frown. "But this is my seat."

My head fell back on a groan at his overprotectiveness. "For the love of God. Just move down! It's not that big of a deal."

After a few seconds, Ethan finally moved, albeit reluctantly, putting me between him and Kevin.

I sat, ignoring the cold metal penetrating my (only slightly too short) skirt and took in his red and white striped shirt and cap, and his black framed glasses and asked, "Where's Waldo?" with a little laugh. "I like it."

"Thanks." His cheeks flushed just a bit as he looked down.

"He looks like a douche," Ethan muttered only loud enough for me and Harlow to hear. I cut a seething look at him over my shoulder before turning back to Kevin with a grin, determined to put Ethan, his overbearing ways, and his too good looks out of my mind while I had a friendly conversation with someone I'd known for years.

"So you like football?"

"Not really," he chuckled. "I'm just here to support

the school. Never really was into sports all that much. I was more about studying than athletics, if you'll remember."

I gave him a smile that promptly turned to grinding teeth when I heard Ethan's quiet chuckle, followed by an equally quiet, "Are you fucking kidding me with this guy?"

"Well that's nice of you," I told him even though it was becoming more and more difficult to ignore the man sitting on my right. As if his behavior wasn't bad enough, the damn man insisted on sitting pressed right up against my side. Only good thing about his invasion of my personal space was that he was warming that side of my body. However, the other half was so cold I was beginning to worry I'd lose feeling in it.

Kevin and I talked more throughout the first two quarters of the game. I'd occasionally get pulled away by the action taking place on the field and lose myself jumping up and down, cheering along with my family and friends for our team whenever they made a touchdown or interception, but to his credit, Kevin just smiled indulgently. It was after our second interception that I sat back down and noticed the appreciative look on his face as he eyed my legs beneath my skirt.

There were no butterflies in my stomach, no sparks

when I looked at Kevin, not like the ones I felt whenever Ethan brushed against me, or leaned over to whisper about a play that just happened in my ear, or even when he pulled me into a hug after a particularly awesome touchdown, but he was a nice enough guy so I didn't want to draw attention to it and risk embarrassing him.

I shivered and turned my eyes back to the field, wrapping my arms around me and rubbing my arms in order to create heat.

"You cold?" Ethan asked, his warm breath skimming across my ear, causing me to shiver again, only this time for a much different reason.

"I'm fine," I lied, not wanting to give him the satisfaction of being right. The brotherly antics were wearing on my very last nerve.

His face was still unnecessarily close as he chuckled. "Liar."

Just then, Kevin chimed in, "If you're cold, I could get you some hot chocolate from the vendor stand."

"Oh." His offer was unexpected but totally welcome, seeing as my insides were beginning to frost. "That would be great. Thank you so much."

"No problem." He stood and gave me another of those shy smiles. "I'll be right back."

"What are you doing, talking to that asshole?" Ethan

asked in a low growl the moment Kevin began descending the bleachers.

My head whipped around to find he was so close we were almost nose to nose. "He's not an asshole," I bit. "He's a sweet guy. Maybe you should pay attention to how he acts. Women actually appreciate that kind of behavior."

His head jerked back slightly. "It's a bullshit act, is what it is. He's playing you."

"You're crazy! He's not playing me!"

"I'd bet my left nut that shy, nice guy shit is all an act just to get in your pants."

"Oh my God!" I shouted, throwing my hands in the air. Luckily, our team just did something on the field to make the whole crowd cheer so my outburst went unnoticed. "This is ridiculous, Ethan. "*You're* the one being an asshole. For your information, Kevin's always been shy. It's how he was all through school."

"Maybe," he shrugged, "but that's not the case now. My guess is he's grown into his looks and knows that awkward-as-fuck blushing shit works on the ladies because most of you are suckers. Trust me, he wants to fuck you."

I wanted to slap him *so bad*. My palm was actually itching for it. "You know what's bullshit? Your overprotective brother routine. *That*'s bullshit! You have no right to judge Kevin when you don't even know him. And newsflash, dickhead. I'm an adult now. I don't need *or want* you wading into my business so you can save my virtue or some shit." Leaning close, I hissed quietly so only he could hear. "My virtue's long gone and has been since junior year in the back seat of Kenneth Randall's Ford Focus. So back the hell off!"

I was too wrapped up in my own anger to notice Ethan's face had turned an alarming shade of red so deep it almost looked purple, or that the muscle in his jaw was ticking like crazy.

"Where the fuck is Randall? I'm going to beat his ass."

"God! Stop! Just stop, okay? I don't need you looking out for me anymore. I don't need a big brother."

"That's what you think I'm doing? Being a big brother?" Something about his tone seemed off.

"Just..." I paused, somewhat losing steam at the sight of his golden colored eyes flashing with something I couldn't quite put my finger on. "Just treat me like you would any of your other friends. You said that's what you wanted, right? To be my friend again?"

"Yes," he all but growled the one word.

"Then act like it."

His eyes closed and his chest rose and fell with a

deep breath before his lids opened and he focused on me once more. "I don't like that guy."

Something in my belly whooshed. and I struggled to decipher if it was a good whoosh or a bad one. The intensity in his gaze and the resoluteness of his words was something I'd never experienced with him before. The actions were the same as how he used to be years ago, but it just... *felt* different.

Doing my best to push it to the back of my mind, I shook my head and replied, "I don't care. It's not up to you who I associate with."

His whispered, *"Fuck,"* came out garbled as he leaned back to run a hand over his face. With his body having moved away from mine, and the tension dwindling, becoming less of a distraction, I shivered again as the cold seeped back in.

"Shit," Ethan grunted. Leaning further away from me, he said something to Chloe that I wasn't able to hear. Seconds later, he straightened, but this time with a fluffy blanket in his hands. "Come here," he said, moving into me.

"What? Why?" Ignoring my instincts, I slid away, needing space between us.

"Just come here, would you? Stop sliding away." One of his arms hooked around my waist and yanked until my side was flush against his.

"What are you doing?" I asked as he shook out the blanket and proceeded to drape it around both our shoulders.

"I'm cold too. Killing two birds with one stone."

"Oh." I couldn't bring myself to pull away again. Not only because the blanket and Ethan's massive body were providing much needed warmth, but because being snuggled under it next to him as he looped his arm back around my waist and held me close just felt... good. Too good. *Dangerously* good. But I was too weak to put a stop to it.

"Here you go," Kevin's cheerful voice called out, pulling me back into reality. When my head turned to face him, I was surprised to see the bewilderment and, if I was reading it correctly, disappointment on his face. Ethan must have noticed it at the same time I did because his arm tightened around me and pulled me closer.

Kevin tried his best to mask the emotions I'd just seen on his face by giving me a somewhat wooden grin. "I didn't realize you two were together."

Oh. "Oh! No! We're not!" My argument came more from a self-preservation standpoint than anything else, because just as I moved away from Ethan's arm every fiber of my body protested against it. "We were just cold and sharing the blanket." The words felt dry in my mouth, heavy on my tongue, but I forced them out since they were the absolute truth.

His smile became less stiff and he sat down next to me and passed me a hot chocolate at the same time Ethan's whole body grew stiff against me.

To say the rest of the game was uncomfortable would have been the understatement of the century.

Chapter Seventeen

Ethan

THAT FUCKER ASKED her out.

Right in front of me. I had to hand it to the guy. He had that nice guy bullshit down pat while still having balls big enough to make a move on Eliza with me sitting Right. *Fucking*. There.

It took every ounce of willpower I had not to knock the guy's teeth down his throat when the game ended and, instead of moving with the rest of the crowd as they began exiting the stadium, he turned and asked Eliza if she'd like to go to dinner with him the following Tuesday.

And she'd hesitated. I *knew* she did, I could feel it when I pressed close to her. She wanted to say no, or at the very least she was uncertain. But because I was a fucking idiot, I'd run my mouth and pushed her, basically leaving her feeling like she had no choice but to say yes, even if it was just to fuck with me.

Which was exactly what she did.

It was already Sunday evening and I was *still* stewing over it, pissed at myself for pushing her when I knew she'd react. Pissed at her for reacting. And pissed at that bastard for encroaching on what I was quickly starting to think of as my territory. On many levels Eliza had always been *mine*. She was my best friend, my confidant, more mine than anyone else's in most of the ways that mattered, and now that I had her back in my life, I struggled to suppress the need to make her mine on *all* levels that mattered.

And now she was going out on a fucking date.

And I wanted to shove my fist through something every time I thought about it. Not the most preferable mood to be in when I was with Harlow and Noah as they took Evan around town to trick-or-treat.

I'd considered turning them down when they asked if I wanted to join them, but keeping myself holed up in their house with only PT with Fletch as my human interaction wasn't doing anything to help my foul mood so I'd agreed. We'd been at it for an hour and a half already, and I'd started to regret my decision, feeling an annoying headache from the masses of screaming kids *everywhere*, when we rounded a corner and I saw her.

"Cate! Abbi!" Evan yelled before taking off their direction, the fake light saber at his side nearly impaling a few kids along the way. There was no stopping the grin that started to tip my lips when Eliza caught sight of me, her eyes going wide, then guarded in an effort to mask the fact that she wasn't sure how to react around me. Any other guy would have considered those shutters she slid into place to be from disinterest, but I knew her better than that, and my gut told me it was something more.

She looked amazing. The faded jeans hugged her legs and hips to perfection, leaving me to believe that they worked the same miracle on her ass. The long sleeve, V-neck t-shirt wasn't anything special, but it was tight enough to dip in at her waist and low enough for just a glimpse of cleavage. Her hair was down and blowing in the soft breeze, and I had no doubt it smelled like almonds and vanilla. At that moment I'd have given anything to bury my face in her hair and inhale. Only thing that would have made it any better was if she were naked, in my bed, underneath me.

"Hey guys," my sister waved as Eliza, along with Chloe, her dad, and her little sisters stopped on the sidewalk next to us. "How's trick-or-treating going so far?"

"I got like, a *million* pieces of candy!" Abbi—who'd

clearly already dipped into her stash—yelled as she held a bulging bag up over her head.

Chloe and Eliza held up large plastic cups with lids and straws as an answer, judging by the color of the liquid inside each they were filled to the brim with red wine.

"Nice," Harlow nodded. "Why don't I ever remember to do that?"

"Because you always know I pack extra," Chloe answered, sliding a backpack off her back and pulling out a thermos.

"And this is why we're best friends," Harlow said as she snatched the thermos from Chloe's hand and chugged.

"I'm a princess," Abbi exclaimed, pulling my attention off her oldest sister and down to her. Her hands held out both sides of her skirt as she swayed side to side to show off the glittery material of her princess dress.

"And a beautiful one at that," I told her with a smile.

"It's not as cool as a cheerleader, but Mommy said Daddy would have a corny...cornair...*cor...in...ary*," she finally managed on her last try.

"And Mommy was right, sweetheart," Derrick answered, pulling her against his leg as he wrapped an arm around her, looking a little pale at just the thought of it.

A snort coming from beside me had me turning to see Eliza trying in vain to stifle a laugh as she sucked on her straw.

I studied her flushed cheeks and the slight glassiness of her gorgeous hazel eyes, and gasped in fake shock. "Eliza Anderson, I can't believe it. You're taking your little sisters trick-or-treating drunk!"

Her cheeks grew redder as she giggled. "I'm not drunk." She so was. "I'm buzzed. I'm just remembering my father's face before we left when I told him I planned on wearing my cheerleader costume to take the girls out tonight." The giggles grew in frequency. "I thought that vein in his forehead was going to burst!" Then she dissolved into laughter, followed quickly by an equally *buzzed* Chloe, and Abbi and Cate who had no clue why they were laughing, but decided to join in on the fun anyway.

"More candy!" Evan yelled like a battle cry, and the girls joined right in, giving us adults no choice but to follow along after them as they ran up to another house to add to their loot.

We walked behind the rest of the crowd in silence for a few houses as Eliza finished off the rest of her wine. I didn't want to be the one to break the silence. The ball was in her court. I'd made stupid mistakes already, and I was determined not to keep making them by pushing her. I wanted to talk to her, to hear her voice, but I was going to wait her out. Luckily, I didn't have to wait long.

"Your knee isn't bothering you walking around on it?"

I glanced over to find her eyes focused on the brace on my leg, her eyebrows dipped in a cute little frown. "You worried about me, sweetheart?"

Her head shot up, gaze meeting mine, and I gave her that grin that had worked in my favor for more years than I could count when it came to women. A grin I learned moments later Eliza was immune to.

"Don't you give me that look," she demanded. "I've seen that look before. I saw it when you were trying to hook up with Peggy Cafferty... and Samantha Williams... and Sherry Line—"

"Okay, okay," I cut her off with a frown of my own. "I get it. No more of *that look*, all right?" She seemed happy enough with that and turned to face ahead. We came to a stop while the kids hit up another house. "And to answer your question, my knee feels fine."

I got her eyes back, which made me really fucking happy. Jesus, how had I never noticed she had the most beautiful eyes I'd ever seen?

"Really?" She sounded skeptical, and I couldn't help but tease.

"You really are worried. Aw, sweetheart. I'm touched."

"Of course I'm worried." The moment the words left her mouth I could tell by the startled look on her face that she hadn't meant to say it out loud. "What I mean is—"

I didn't want to give her a chance to backtrack, so I wrapped my arm around her shoulder, enjoying the feel of her pressed against my side as we started to walk again, and said, "I appreciate that, Eliza. I really do."

We walked in silence for a while before she spoke again. "Well... I know how much football means to you. I can only imagine how you felt when it happened."

I let out a quick bark of laughter. "I'll tell you. It was fucking excruciating. I was scared to look down, thinking the lower half of my leg was just dangling there. Christ, I'd broken bones growing up that hurt less."

"That's not what I meant," she said softly, looking at the sidewalk. I took it as a good sign that she still hadn't pulled away.

I gave her hair a tug to get her gaze back and asked quietly, "Then what'd you mean, honey?"

"Just that... football's your life. You had to have been scared when you got hurt. It means everything to you."

Her words caused me to come to an abrupt halt, pulling her to a stop with me. I scanned her face, seeing nothing but sincerity glistening in her hazel eyes. "Not everything," I told her, meaning those two words from the very depth of me.

Something passed between us right then, something I'd never experienced before, something so intense my chest tightened and my stomach lurched. I was so sure she was going to acknowledge what was happening between us just then that made the air feel like it was full of electricity. I *hoped* she would.

But she cleared her throat, pulled from my arm, and started walking again. Only this time, her fingers stayed clasped in front of her so I couldn't have taken her hand if I wanted to... which I did. Not that I could have since there really was no reason to hold her hand that wouldn't have sent her running in the other direction.

We didn't speak again as my nephew and her sisters finally seemed to be winding down, indicating trick-or-treating was coming to an end. I wasn't ready for it and was just about to turn to tell her so and ask her to go get a drink or something, when she beat me to the punch.

"This was kind of nice," she said, catching me off guard. "I mean us actually being in each other's company and not fighting or yelling at each other."

I smiled again, this time making sure it didn't hold a hint of *the look*. "It really was." I opened my mouth to suggest we head over to The Moose when she continued looking toward our families.

"Looks like we're done for the night. You should head home and ice your knee or something. You know, to make sure it's okay from all this walking."

Shit, it felt like I'd just been punched in the gut. My smile dropped a little "Uh, yeah. You're probably right."

"Well, seeing as we have this truce between us now, I won't dread seeing you next time." She reached up and nudged my shoulder, and with her next words my smile completely died. "Unless you pull that brotherly shit again."

All I could manage was a low, emotionless, "Yeah," as she began walking backwards.

"I'm sure I'll see you around. Have a good night." She started to turn, but called over her shoulder, "Oh! And rest that knee."

With that she waved and took off with the rest of her family, leaving me and mine behind.

A wave.

A fucking wave. Not even so much as a hug.

Looked like I still have my work cut out for me after all.

Chapter Eighteen

Ethan

SINCE MY RETURN to Pembrooke, my days had been filled with therapy, shitty daytime TV, and sitting on my ass at Sinful Sweets Café, hoping to catch a glimpse of Eliza. To say I was bored out of my mind would have been putting it mildly, so when Quinn called and asked if I wanted to grab a beer with him at The Moose and catch the football game on their big screens, there was no way in hell I was turning him down. It would give me some much needed adult interaction. Not to mention the fact that it was Tuesday evening and Eliza was more than likely already out on her *date*.

Just thinking about that set my teeth on edge.

The evening crowd was still going strong by the time I walked through the door. The place was a little more than half full as I scanned the faces. Out of the corner of my eye I saw Quinn's hand come up to grab my attention. I gave him a chin lift and started toward the booth he'd snagged returning several greetings — some from people I knew, some from people I couldn't remember ever seeing before — as I made my way over.

"Hey man, glad you could make it," he said once I'd shrugged out of my light weight jacket and slid into the bench across from him.

"You and me both, dude. If I hadn't gotten out of that house soon I was liable to lose my fucking mind."

He chuckled and lifted his beer bottle to his lips as a waitress stopped to take my drink order. A few minutes later, I leaned back, relaxed with a bottle of bud in my hand. "So, how'd you manage a night out with your little girl at home?"

He gave me a funny look. It wasn't necessarily bad, just very speculative. "See you didn't jump to the conclusion she'd be home with her mom, so I'm taking that as you already know that particular story?"

I gave it to him straight. "I know she's passed. Don't know how and don't plan on asking. That's your story to share if or when you're in the mood. I didn't come here tonight to get in your business. I just came for good beer, good company, and hopefully some good wings. I'm starving."

His appreciation showed as his mouth twitched before he took another pull of his beer. "Good to know. That conversations for another, *much later* time when I don't have a shift at the station the next day and have the opportunity to get drunk out of my goddamn mind. And to answer your earlier question, my girl's with my folks. They like to keep her for sleepovers one night a week and every other weekend. She gets time with her Meemaw and Papaw, they get to spoil their grandbaby, and I get a breather which means I get my bed to myself without having to worry about being kicked in the ribs or punched in the junk because my baby has a habit of climbing in with me in the middle of the night and flails in her sleep. Works for everyone."

"Sounds like it." I laughed because he didn't sound put out in the slightest with his nightly beatings. "What's her name?"

"Sophia," he answered with a smile, telling me his little girl meant everything to him. It sucked that he'd lost his wife in whatever way he lost her. I hated that for him. It had been a long while since we'd hung out, but he was a good guy back then, and proof showed he was still a good guy now. So, in spite of the hurt he suffered with losing his wife, I was glad he had good in the form of a little girl that lit his face up with just the mere mention of her.

We shot the shit for a while, ordering a couple baskets of wings and another round. He asked about my knee, but didn't push the subject, digging into it like the media had right after it happened.

"So... Eliza, huh?" he asked after we'd finished our second round and had begun our third.

"What are you talking about?"

A shit-eating grin took over his face. "Man, I saw you when you thought I was putting the moves on her. Thought you were two seconds away from kicking my ass right there in the middle of the restaurant. I remember you guys being tight, but that wasn't what that look spelled out."

"Things with that are... complicated," I understated vaguely.

"How so?"

It was a simple question that got my back up, not because I felt like it wasn't any of his business, but because the answer shed even more light on the glaringly obvious fact that my current situation with Eliza was all my goddamned fault.

"In the sense that I bailed six years ago, basically telling her she was just an immature kid I was done wasting my time with, and never looked back... not until now, at least."

He whistled low. "Wow. Yeah, brother. I'd say that's seriously complicated. You planning on apologizing?"

I shot him a look. "You really think I haven't done that already?"

His smile told me he was getting more than just a little enjoyment out of my predicament in the way all men who weren't having to suffer through woman problems did. "Well, I wouldn't think you were enough of a prick to treat her like that in the first place, seeing as everyone in town knew you two were tight. You'll have to excuse me for thinking you might still be that same shit-for-brains."

I let out a surprised laugh at his bluntness. "Yeah, man. I've apologized. At least ten times by my last count."

Quinn rested back against the booth, throwing his free hand along the top of it. "Well, if I know Eliza—and most people here do since she's lived here almost her entire life—I think it's safe to say that woman doesn't have it in her to hold a grudge for very long. If you're really sorry, I'm sure she'll forgive you."

I let out a breath and ran a hand over my face. "She's already starting to," I admitted, not feeling the least bit better with the knowledge that at least she didn't still hate me. "It took a while, but she's getting there."

"Then why do you look like someone's just pissed in your corn flakes?"

"Because she's on a fucking date," I growled in answer, the hand holding my beer bottle squeezing tight around the cool glass.

"Ah," Quinn said with a knowing tone to his voice. "And it's been six years since you've seen her. I'm guessing it's not lost on you that Eliza Anderson's all grown up, and done it in a real good way. That friendship you used to feel for her has turned into something else all together."

I glared at the humor lacing through his words. "Glad my suffering can amuse you, asshole." Then something else about his comment registered. "And I *knew* you were checking her out that day at the restaurant, you fucker."

He laughed long and hard. "Relax, would you? I'm not interested in her like that, she's a friend, but I'm not dead or blind either. Any man with a pulse can see the woman's hot as shit."

He was right about that. I couldn't blame him for noticing... as long as he didn't touch. "I'm in a seriously screwed up way right now, and I've got no one to blame but myself. And to make matters worse, the only reason she agreed to the fucking date with this other guy was to push my buttons because she thought I was acting like an overbearing brotherly figure."

"Shit," Quinn chuckled. "Never thought I'd say this, but I'm so glad I'm not you right now."

I couldn't fault him. Hell, if I had a friend in the same shoes as me, I'd be laughing at his expense too. "Thanks, dickhead."

We hung out a while longer and had just finished paying our tab when something over my shoulder caught Quinn's attention. "Well, it was good hanging out man. I gotta get home and get some shut eye, but you might want to stick around for a little while longer."

"Why's that?"

The smile on his face was so damn big it nearly split his face in two. "Because your girl's walking in with her date."

Jerking around in the booth, my eyes trailed in on the direction his had been pointed, and sure enough, that Where's Waldo son of a bitch was holding the door open for Eliza to pass through. The smile on his face was huge, like he was sixteen years old and had just nailed the prom queen. But as she turned to thank him, I saw it, and I knew in my gut that hers was forced. I didn't need to keep track of her these past six years to know that wasn't one of her real smiles. I'd seen the *real* thing a million times. I'd earned a thousand of them myself, I'd know her real smile from a mile away with one eye closed. And that was *not* what she was giving him.

"Take it you're staying?"

"Oh yeah," I answered, not taking my eyes off the two of them as he placed his hand on the small of her back and led her to a vacant table on the other side of the bar. At the sight of his hand on her, my own clenched again, so tight I was surprised the bottle in my hand didn't shatter. Lifting it to my lips, I downed the rest of its contents in one gulp. She took off her jacket and my head just about exploded. "And I think I'll be needing more of these." She looked good. Too good. At least for the dick head she was with. The navy sweater dress she was wearing hugged her curves like it had been made for her, her ass... *Jesus.* Her feet were encased in tan high-heeled boots that went up to her knees and made her legs look fucking phenomenal. *I* wanted to be the one touching her while she wore that killer dress. Or any time, really. And I wanted to stomp across the bar and plant my fist in that asshole's face before taking what — had I not fucked everything up—should have been mine.

"Well, whatever you do, don't make an ass out of yourself," Quinn warned giving me a pat on the back. "Her Sherriff dad might not be all that forgiving when you finally decide to make your play for his little girl."

"I'll take that under advisement." I returned his chin

lift as he headed for the door and disappeared out it a few seconds later.

Deciding I needed a better vantage point, I moved from the booth to the bar, taking up one of the stools so I could keep their table in my line of sight as I ordered another beer — only this time I got a shot of tequila to chase it down with. Then I settled in and waited, hoping to God it wasn't going to be a long night.

Chapter Nineteen

Eliza

I MADE A mistake.

I never should have agreed to a date with Kevin. It wasn't that he wasn't a nice guy. He really was great. My heart just wasn't in it, so what should have been a fun, enjoyable evening was more akin to a checkup at the dentist's office — relatively painless, but still something I'd rather not have to deal with.

Dinner had been nice, but that was the extent of it. Just... nice. I engaged in conversation when required, and did my best to appear to be paying attention when he spoke, but throughout the entire evening my mind kept wandering to a place it shouldn't, or more correctly to a *person*. And no matter how hard I tried not to think about Ethan, my stupid brain just kept conjuring him up.

All night long.

When Kevin picked me up and told me I looked beautiful, I wondered what it would have felt like if it had been Ethan picking me up for our first date, saying those words to me.

When he rested his palm on my back to lead me into the restaurant, I wondered what it would feel like for Ethan to touch me like that. Would I have felt a bolt of electricity like I had when he touched me on Halloween?

When Kevin ordered his meal, I wondered if that was something Ethan would have liked to eat, and when he suggested drinks at The Moose because he wasn't ready for the evening to end, I'd stupidly thought about whether or not Ethan would have gone in for a kiss after the end of a first date.

It was pathetic. It was idiotic. It made me angry because Kevin certainly deserved better.

"Eliza? You okay?" At the sound of Kevin's voice, my attention snapped back to our table at The Moose.

God, could I have sucked any worse?

"I'm so sorry," I apologized with a guilty smile. "My mind must have wandered. What were you saying?"

He looked at me with a kind, yet concerned expression. "You okay? You've seemed a little distracted tonight."

"What? Of course!" I lied, my voice rising a little too high. "I'm totally fine. So what were you saying?"

His expression changed but the smile remained. "Eliza, it's okay," he said softly. "I'm not an idiot. I know you haven't been into tonight. I'd hoped coming here would've loosened you up a bit, but I can see now I was wrong. And that's all right." And the fact that he sounded so genuine, so understanding, hurt. I. Was. *Awful.*

And yes, it was obvious I *could* suck worse, because not only was Kevin a great guy, but I couldn't even fake it well enough for him to believe I'd been interested all night.

"God," I rested my elbows on the table and dropped my head into my hands. "I'm so sorry. I suck. I'm the worst person ever."

I heard his soft laughter at the same time I felt his fingers wrap gently around my wrists, pulling them away from my face. "You're not the worst person ever."

"I am!" I cried.

His chuckle grew a touch louder. "You're not. You're just into someone else. I suspected as much when I asked you out at the football game, but I took the chance anyway, knowing it might not have gone in my favor."

At that my back went stiff. "I don't know what you're talking about. There's no one else."

He gave me a look that said *who are you kidding.* "Okay. Let's just say you're not into someone else."

"Because I'm not!"

"I believe you." He nodded, even though he so didn't believe me.

"See?!" I all but shouted. "Gah! You're so... you're so nice!"

In spite of knowing the night had in fact *not* gone in his favor, he still laughed and smiled like being shot down was just water that ran right off his back. "You say that like it's a bad thing."

"It is! Well... it's not really. It's actually pretty great. But it would just make me feel so much better if you'd maybe not be so nice to me."

His eyes grew comically wide just before he burst into laughter. "You'd rather I be mean to you just because we didn't make a love connection?"

I sat back in my chair and crossed my arms over my chest, my face taking on a pout. "Well when you put it like that it just sounds ridiculous."

Kevin's laughter finally died down and he rested his clasped hands on the table. "Look, I asked you out because I thought you were interesting and I wanted a chance to get to know you more. You were always nice in high school, and you're *still* nice now. We didn't hit it off romantically. But I still enjoyed your company."

"I enjoyed yours too," I replied honestly. Because I had. He'd made me laugh and, despite my thoughts being full of Ethan, not once was I bored in Kevin's company.

"If it makes you feel better, silver lining is I'm not going to go home and pine after you, so there's no reason we can't be friends."

My face curved into a genuine smile. "I'd really, really like that."

"Then it's settled." He clapped his palm on the table. "From here on out we're friends."

I giggled and nodded in agreement just as a crash rattled so loud in my ears that I jumped in my chair and both Kevin and I twisted our heads around toward the bar area. "*Shit,*" I whispered as soon as my eyes hit the scene. The crash came from a waitress who'd just dropped an entire tray of drinks. A tray she dropped because someone had apparently stumbled into her. "*Shit,*" I whispered again when Ethan's gaze came to mine and I could see that he hadn't stumbled because of his injured knee. He'd stumbled because he was three sheets to the wind.

And he was now coming our way.

"Do you need me to get you out of here?" Kevin asked, but it was a few seconds too late. Ethan moved surprisingly fast for someone recovering from an ACL surgery *and* being completely smashed.

"Waldo." The one word came out as a growl as he stared Kevin down.

"Ethan." At the sound of my voice, his head turned, his eyes trailing behind by a second, laying proof to just how drunk he was, not that I couldn't already smell the alcohol on him. "What are you doing?"

"What? A guy can't have a few beers with a friend?" he asked sarcastically.

"You're drunk. And it smells like you've had a lot more than just beer. You shouldn't be drinking anything else."

A bark of humorless laughter rumbled from his chest as he stumbled on his feet, having to drop his hands to the top of the table to keep his balance. "You acting like you actually care about me now?" The question cut me because I never *stopped* caring.

"Stop it," I whispered, my voice full of warning.

"I think maybe we should get you a cab home, friend," Kevin cut in. He was just beginning to stand, his hands out like he was reaching to help steady Ethan. God, he was *such* a nice guy.

"We're not friends," Ethan bit out so harshly Kevin paused. "You have what I want. As long as that's the case, we'll never be friends."

I felt my eyes go round in shock, not only at the malice in his voice as he spoke, but at the confusing declaration. What the hell was he even talking about?

"Ethan, enough," I broke the stare-off happening between the two men by standing from my chair. "You aren't even making any sense, and you're causing a scene. Just let Kevin get you a cab."

"I don't need *Kevin* to do anything for me." With that, he turned his back on me and continued talking, moving closer to Kevin in a way that didn't seem good. "You're lucky enough to keep her, you better fucking treat her like gold."

"Ethan, stop!" I snapped.

To his credit, Kevin stood his ground, even though his face was two shades paler. I couldn't really blame him for being scared of Ethan. The man had at least two inches and several pounds of muscle on him. His hands came up in a placating gesture. "I think the two of you should probably talk once you've sobered up.

"Don't need to sober up," Ethan told him. "I'm talking now, and I'm talking to *you*." To emphasize his point, he drilled his finger into Kevin's chest, making him wince.

"Enough!" I jumped in and grabbed Ethan's hand, shoving it away from Kevin. "You're embarrassing yourself *and* me!"

But he wasn't done. "Fucked up six years ago. Fucked up so goddamned bad I lost the best thing in my life. You do that you're even more stupid than I am." The air in the entire room grew thick at the same time my back shot straight and every muscle in my body froze up.

"Ethan," Kevin coaxed. How he managed to sound so calm was beyond me, because I suddenly felt like the ground beneath my feet was crumbling. "Let's get you home, okay? Stop now before you say something you can't take back tomorrow. You don't want to do this when you're drunk."

"Lost her," Ethan mumbled more to himself than anyone else. "And I fucking hate myself for it. Every goddamned day for the past six years. And I'll hate myself for the rest of my life 'cause I'll never get her back. Not the way I had her then, and not the way I want her now."

I couldn't listen anymore. I just couldn't. It was all just too much. What he'd said, the ravaged expression on his face when he'd said it. I was at war with myself. Part of me wanting to grab hold of him and hold on for dear life, the other part wanted to hurt him for letting me go in the first place, for wrecking me.

His words filled me with joy, yet at the same time they destroyed me.

Because I felt the exact same way.

I wanted him in a way I never had before, not even when I was ten years old and convinced I would someday marry him. But I couldn't trust him not to break me again. When he left the first time, it killed. The pain was worse than anything my own mother had ever done to me because he'd been my *best friend*. There was no way I'd ever survive him leaving a second time.

And he *would* leave. It was a guarantee. His life wasn't in Pembrooke anymore. It was in Denver.

I grabbed my jacket from the back of my chair and snatched my purse off the table. The air was too thick. I couldn't breathe. I was feeling too much of everything and if I didn't get out now, I'd crumble in front of everyone. "I'm sorry. I have to go," I mumbled, pushing past the two men in front of me, ignoring their calls and all the eyes of the bar customers on me as I bolted for the door.

Chapter Twenty

Eliza

"Eliza! Eliza, wait!"

I didn't wait. The wooden boards of the sidewalk clanked angrily under my high-heeled boots as I rushed to get home. I was only about halfway there by the time Ethan caught up with me.

"Go home, Ethan!" I yelled over my shoulder, never breaking stride.

"Damn it! Will you just fucking slow down? I need to talk to you."

"I have nothing to say to you! You had no right to say that shit back there! Just leave me alone!"

"I'm not leaving you alone until you talk to me!"

"God!" I stopped just long enough to spin around and pin him with a hateful look. "There's nothing to talk about! You can't just disappear for six years, then come back and say... all that," I waved my hand back in the direction of The Moose. "You have no right!"

"Baby, please—"

"Don't call me that! I'm not your baby."

I picked up the pace, my feet moving me faster as I rounded the side of the building that led to the alley behind the cafe. I was almost home free. Rummaging through my purse for my keys, my foot just hit the bottom step that would take me up to my apartment when Ethan's pained voice made me jolt to a stop.

"ARGH! Goddamn it! *Fuck!*"

I spun around just in time to see him hunch over, his hands to the knee that was still covered by the brace. At the sight of it, my insides went cold and everything that had happened earlier to make me run flew from my mind.

I dropped my purse on the ground and ran straight toward him. "Oh my God. Are you okay?" I put my hand to his shoulders to help straighten him. His eyelids were screwed shut, his face twisted in pain as his chest rose and fell with uneven breaths. "Christ, Ethan. What happened?"

"My knee," he panted. "Wrenched it."

My stomach dropped. "Shit. Okay, okay. Just breathe." I leaned into him and took some of his weight. "Are you going to be okay? Did you tear it again?"

"No," he answered, his breathing finally beginning to slow down. "No. It'll be okay. Just twisted it."

"Jesus," I said on an exhale, relief and frustration warring inside of me. "Have you lost your mind?" I snapped, frustration winning out as I led him closer to the stairs. "You could have really hurt yourself, you dumbass!"

He limped slowly, leaning on me to keep weight off his bad knee. "I needed to talk to you, and you wouldn't slow down."

"So you risked a potential career ending injury. Really fucking smart, Ethan."

He wobbled slightly, the effects of the booze still in his system. "I hate it when you're mad at me," he muttered as I propped him up against the wall at the base of the stairs.

"Then stop doing stupid shit and I wouldn't have to keep getting mad," I seethed as I moved away from him to get to my purse. There was no way I was getting him up those stairs all by myself. And putting him in my car and driving him back to Harlow and Noah's would have just prolonged a night that I was ready to be done with.

"Always doing stupid shit," he continued to mumble as I rummaged in my bag for my phone. "Why couldn't I have just been content with my life here?" My hand froze at his question, and I had to squeeze my eyes shut against the onslaught of tears that threatened to break free. I'd asked myself that same question over and over for so long, that hearing him actually voice it was like a physical blow. I gave myself a few seconds to compose myself before I continued the search for my phone. Unfortunately, Ethan used my silence to continue his goddamned self-reflection.

"If I could have just been happy, I would still have you. Why was I always such a miserable fucking person?"

He was ripping me apart. If he didn't stop soon, I wasn't sure how much of me there would have been left. I'd never been so confused in my life. I could have shouted in relief when my fingers curled around my cellphone for the simple fact I wouldn't have to listen to him say things that made my belly curl with pleasure at the same time fury brought my blood to a boil.

"'Lo?" Lilly's sleepy voice said on the other end. I was lucky she answered since my roommate slept like the dead.

"Hey, it's me. I need your help. Can you come outside?"

"What? Where are you?"

I twisted my head to look in Ethan's direction when

he let out a pitiful groan. "I'm outside. Just come downstairs." I hung up and dropped the phone back into my purse in just enough time to dash back to Ethan and grab him as he toppled over sideways.

"What the hell?" Lilly spoke from the landing.

"Come help me," I groaned as I tried to carry too much of his weight. I was only seconds away from falling on my ass. "I can't get him upstairs by myself."

"Good Lord," she grunted as she reached us and threw one of his arms over her shoulder. "He smells like a brewery."

We began the tedious process of getting Ethan up the stairs and into the apartment. "I know. He got wasted at the Moose and made a huge scene. Then the stupid jerk twisted his knee chasing after me."

"Mmm," Ethan moaned, turning his head and burying his face in my hair just as we made it to the landing. "Always smell so good."

"Oh my god," Lilly's entire body began shaking with laughter, causing my hold on Ethan to slip.

"Shut up," I grumbled, wrapping my arm tighter around his waist to keep steady. The move only made him bury his face further into my neck. He moaned and inhaled deeply, causing goosebumps to break out across my flesh.

"Fuck baby," he groaned into my hair. "Never get tired of your smell."

"Shit, Eliza. How much did he have to drink?"

We made it all the way into the living room. "I don't know," I strained and dropped his massive frame onto the couch. "Enough to start spouting out stupid stuff in front of every single person at The Moose."

Lilly and I both stood, staring down at his prone body on the couch, both of us panting for breath, our hands resting on our hips. "So what are we supposed to do with him now?"

"I guess we'll just let him sleep it off. He can call his sister tomorrow when he wakes up."

I leaned down and pulled off his shoes one by one before lifting his lower legs as gently as I could onto the couch so Ethan was lying down instead of sitting up at a weird, uncomfortable looking angle. I hadn't even stood back up when his hands were suddenly on my hips and I was moving with a startled yelp.

"Ethan!"

He moaned again as his strong arms held me against his body. I squirmed and pushed, trying to get off from on top of him, but one arm locked around my back while the other trailed down my side, causing my body to lock up as it got closer and closer to my ass. "Feel so good," he mumbled with his eyes closed, sounding drowsy.

Two seconds later my body came unlocked when I was proven right and Ethan released a soft, rumbling snore that rattled through his chest and into mine. I put my hands to his massive chest and gave a gentle push only to be thwarted when his arms around me tightened and he shifted in his sleep, twisting his body enough to pin half of mine to the couch beneath him.

"Lilly," I whispered. "Lilly, help me."

I turned my head when I heard a gargled choking sound and found my best friend holding her hands over her mouth to try and suppress her laughter. "This isn't funny," I hissed and struggled against Ethan in vain. "I can't get out. Help me."

"Oh my God," Lilly wheezed, her hands dropping to her knees as she lost it. "This is too good." Then, to my dismay, she disappeared for a few seconds, only to reappear with her phone in her hand.

"What the hell are you doing?"

"Taking a picture. I have to record this moment for posterity."

"Oh, you're such a bitch." I gave his chest another shove and earned even more of his weight as he pulled me further beneath him.

The shutter on her phone's camera clicked a few times before she finally lowered it. "Well, I'm beat. I'm heading back to bed. Sleep tight, you cuddle bugs."

"Lilly, no. Lilly!" I hissed when the light in the living room was extinguished.

"Nighty, night," she called.

"I hate you!"

Then the apartment grew silent, with the exception of Ethan's gentle snoring. It most definitely wasn't the most comfortable position to be in, but every time I tried to move, his hold on me just grew stronger so I was finally forced to stop struggling.

I tried my best to settle in and closed my eyes, only for them to shoot open again when his hips shifted and pressed against mine. His groan sounded almost pained as the stiffness of his erection pressed into me, causing my breath to hitch. "Mmm, feel so good, baby," he snuffled, sleepily, telling me he was still asleep. His face pressed into my neck as he continued to sleep talk. "Miss you, sweetheart." My chest caved in as all the air left my lungs. "Miss you so much."

I remained silent as Ethan's body finally settled completely. The minutes ticked by as he slept like the dead. All the while I was stuck staring up at the dark ceiling, sleep evading me as so many unanswered questions swam through my head.

The most important one being: what the hell was I going to do?

Because no matter how many times I told myself I

wasn't going to let my heart get involved again the truth was, it already was.

There wasn't a doubt in my mind I was going to get hurt again. And the scariest thing about that was there was no way for me to brace for the impact.

Chapter Twenty-One

Ethan

THE NAGGING THROB in my head only grew worse as the sun lit behind my eyelids, pushing away the last dregs of sleep.

Three things hit me all at once. First was that I wasn't on the sleeper sofa in my sister's living room. Second was that, despite the headache, I felt like I'd had one of the best night's sleeps in my entire life. And third, I was surrounded by Eliza's scent, a scent so strong the only thing that could cut through it was the aroma of bacon drifting into the room.

Pushing up to sitting, I took in my surroundings as images of the night before came back to me in full force. It was a curse and a boon, the fact that no matter how drunk I got, I was still able to remember what had happened the night before, and in the case of last night, there were good and bad things about remembering it all. The bad was that I'd once again pissed Eliza off. The good was I remembered how it felt when her warm, lush body was in my arms before I finally succumbed to sleep.

That particular memory was one I was going to enjoy the minute I got myself into a shower. If I didn't, there was no telling how long the hard-on behind my fly would plague me.

"Well, good morning, sleepy head." My head shot around to look over the back of the couch. Lilly stood in the open-concept kitchen, tongs in hand as she manned a skillet full of bacon. "I was wondering how long you'd stay passed out on our couch. Got worried for a second when you didn't move when I kicked you. Had to hold a mirror under your nose just to make sure you were breathing."

I felt relatively confident, by the smile on her face, that she hadn't really kicked me. But I couldn't be positive.

"What time is it?" I asked, reaching into my pocket for my cell. When I came up empty, Lilly spoke again and pointed the tongs in my direction.

"It's on the coffee table. Don't worry. I didn't feel you up when I pulled it out of your pocket. But that damn thing has been ringing off the hook since seven this morning. It was either put it on silent or tap dance on it."

I grabbed it off the table and hit the button at the bottom to turn it on. Sure enough, my phone was on vibrate and there were a ton of missed calls and text messages. All from Harlow worrying about where I was.

"Shit." I fell back on the couch and rubbed my face with my free hand. I shot Harlow a quick text to tell her I was alive and that I'd slept on Eliza's couch the night before. Then it hit me. "Where's Eliza?" I asked as I looked around the room, a sudden sense of dread twisting my stomach into knots at the fact I went to sleep with her and woke up alone.

Lilly studied me for a while before finally responding. "How much do you remember from last night?"

I dropped my phone back on the table and used both hands to scrub my face. "All of it," I answered honestly. After my performance the night before, honesty was the only option I had. With how I'd acted in The Moose and after when I followed her home, I knew I wouldn't have a leg to stand on if I claimed memory loss. Especially after everything I'd said. I needed to talk to her. Finally admit the truth and hope she didn't kick me out on my ass.

"Relax, she's at the café. Her mornings usually start

early. She had to escape your clutches to get her butt down there on time."

Relief slammed into me like a battering ram, and without thought, I was on my feet. "Hey!" Lilly called as I headed for the front door. "You forgot your phone!"

I instantly backtracked and snatched it up from where I'd left it seconds before. "Good luck," she called. "You're seriously going to need it, buddy. But if it's any consolation, I'm rooting for you. Oh! And take the interior stairs! They'll get you right to the kitchen." She pointed in the direction I needed to go.

"Thanks!" I called back just before the door closed behind me. Surprisingly, the pain in my knee wasn't all that bad as I made my way down the stairs. I counted that as a blessing seeing as I could have done irreparable damage last night, had Eliza not been there to help me.

I'd just made it to the base of the stairs when I heard the faint sound of music coming from down the hall. I followed the sound until I came to a swinging door on my right. I pushed in and the sound of Hozier became clearer, along with Eliza humming along with the song. She was all alone in the large kitchen, lost in whatever she was doing and hadn't heard me enter. I caught her in profile and her beauty hit me full force, even standing there in nothing but a pair of jeans and a plain white t-shirt covered in an apron, her hair in a ratty bun at the top of her head and her face clean of all makeup, she was more beautiful than any woman I'd ever seen.

"Hey."

At the sound of my voice, the spoon she was using to stir something in a pot on the stove shot up, slinging something red everywhere as she jumped around on a sharp, startled inhale. "God, Ethan!" she breathed, putting her hand to her chest. "You scared the shit out of me. What are you doing here?"

I didn't hesitate in diving right in. We'd been dancing around each other since the moment I saw her standing in the chip aisle of Mabel's Corner Market. "We need to talk."

"About what?" she asked, feigning ignorance as she turned back to the stove and continued stirring, like she wasn't well aware that I was talking about everything I'd said to her the night before.

"You know damn good and well what we need to talk about," I ground out, my irritation rising with every second that she refused to meet my eyes.

She shrugged. "Far as I'm concerned there's nothing to talk about. I'm busy right now, so you can let yourself out."

"That's bullshit, and you know it."

She never stopped stirring. "It's not. You were drunk

out of your mind and were rambling incoherently. Let's just pretend last night never happened."

Wrong thing to say. "Goddamn it," I seethed. Storming over to the stove, I threw the dial to kill the flame beneath the pot and yanked the spoon out of her hand, throwing it clear across the room.

"*What* is your problem?!" she shouted, spinning around so we were face to face.

"My problem is that you're full of shit!" I shouted back, finally getting a reaction other than indifference from her. And seeing that reaction fed a hunger inside me to push her for more.

"*I'm* full of shit? Are you fucking kidding me?! You're *such* an asshole, Ethan! Not that I should be surprised," she laughed bitterly. "You seem to be making a habit out of that."

I took a step back and pulled in a breath in an attempt to calm down. "Look. We need to talk about what I said last night."

"I don't want to talk about it. You were drunk and talking out of your ass. It didn't mean anything." she declared with finality.

Oh fuck that. All calm flew out the window. Moving back in, I pinned her hips to the counter and rested my hands on either side of her. "Oh, baby. That's where you're wrong. I might have been drunk, but I fucking meant *everything*."

Her chest rose and fell in what most people would have thought was rage. But I knew that pink currently darkening her cheeks was from something else altogether. "Step back."

"Not until you stop with this bullshit and *listen* to me," I hissed. I watched as her hazel eyes flashed with fear coupled with a longing so extreme I felt it in every fiber of my body before it traveled down to my dick, causing it to twitch. I fed off that look like a man trapped in the desert who'd stumbled onto an oasis.

"Ethan. Step. Back."

"Eliza—"

"No!" She shoved at my chest so hard I had no choice but to step back on one foot to stay upright. "No! You don't get to come in here and demand I listen to what you have to say! You don't get to come back into my life after *six fucking years* and turn everything upside down! I was doing fine without you. You do *not* get to do this!"

"I told you why I left!" I fought back, desperation churning my blood.

"And your reasoning was the most selfish thing I've ever heard!" she fired back. "No one, not a single fucking one of us would have asked you to give up your dream to stay here! That was all in *your* head. Everything that happened was your choice. You *chose* to bail instead of talking to your sister about what was bothering you. You *chose* to push everyone who cared about you away. And you *chose* to treat me like I meant *nothing* to you so you didn't have any strings left tying you back to this place. That was all on you, Ethan, not me! You can't just come here and force yourself back into my life after how your treated me. Things have changed. You can't act like the past six years never happened. You threw me away!"

"Because I was in love with you!" I roared, the words bubbling to the surface before I even had a chance to think.

She blinked up at me for several seconds before whispering in a pained voice, "What?"

"Jesus Christ!" I stepped away from her and began pacing the length of the kitchen, my hands pulling at my hair. I'd come this far already, there really was no going back. I was the one that wanted everything out in the open. That meant no more lies. "I was in love with you. You were sixteen fucking years old, Eliza! Do you have any clue how that fucks with a guy's head? I loved you, but I couldn't have you."

"Stop."

I didn't stop. "I wasn't lying when I told you I'd

started considering giving it all up to stay here with you. But it wasn't because you were my best friend."

"Stop."

"You were just a kid, for Christ's sake! I was twenty-two. I couldn't have you no matter how badly I wanted you, and I knew, I fucking *knew* in my bones that if I didn't let you go, I'd lose everything I'd worked my ass off for." I moved back to her so fast it caught her off guard. "But don't think for one goddamned second that it didn't kill me to do what I did to you. It ripped my fucking heart out when you told me you hated me."

"Stop." Her voice grew stronger, but I was lost in my own memory. Remembering that day was like picking at a scab that hadn't quite healed over.

"I made a mistake. I hurt you because I thought I had no other choice, and I'll regret that every day for the rest of my life. But not one day has passed where my feelings for you changed. I loved you back then, and I still love you now."

"*Stop!*" she shrieked, pushing at my chest. "Stop! *Stopstopstop!*" Each word was punctuated by a slap or a hit. "You don't get to say that to me! You threw me away. *You threw me away!*"

"Eliza," I spoke softly, grabbing her wrists as she continued to struggle. "Baby, shh. Calm down." The tears streaming down her cheeks gutted me. I would have given my life to take her pain away.

"You're worse than my mother! You don't know what love is." She continued to fight my hold, getting in any hit she could. Restraining her wasn't helping so I did the only thing I could think to calm her down. The one thing I'd wanted to do for the past six years. The instant my lips hit hers, the fight drained from her. Her body locked up tight for just a second before it melted against me. As soon as I knew she was done fighting, my hands released her wrists and moved to tangle in her hair, tilting her head so I could get deeper. Her soft lips, smooth tongue, that intoxicating smell of vanilla and almond coupled with her exquisite taste, a taste I never thought I'd have, was too much. I let go of her head with one hand and wrapped it around her waist, pinning her body against mine so close not even light could get through as I devoured her mouth.

Her moan slid down my throat, and I was completely lost. I never wanted to be found. I never wanted to stop kissing Eliza. And I was never letting her go again.

Or at least that's what I told myself.

Because the second someone coughed from behind us, she jumped out of my arms like I'd just burned her.

"Sorry, didn't mean to interrupt." We both turned to

look at the man who'd just interrupted, the very same man I was seconds away from murdering.

Eliza cleared her throat and gave the remorseful looking guy a shaky smile as she reached up to fix the ponytail I'd destroyed. "It's fine, Gary. You weren't interrupting."

"The fuck he wasn't," I growled, causing *Gary* to pale. He should have been scared.

Eliza skewered me with a look before saying, very pointedly "Ethan was just leaving."

"Holy shit," Gary said on an exhale. "You're Ethan Prewitt."

"I am,"

"Dude! I'm a *huge* fan! *Huge!* Do you think I could get your autograph?"

"Sure." I offered him a grin, my homicidal tendencies lessening at the realization he was a fan. Reaching out to take the crumpled receipt and pen he'd just pulled from his pocket, I scribbled my name down and handed it back.

"So cool," he breathed.

I looked back at Eliza and saw she looked like her head was only seconds away from exploding. Knowing that getting into another shouting match in front of one of her employees wouldn't win me any brownie points, I decided it was best to leave the remainder of our conversation for another time in the not too distant future.

"We'll finish this later," I mumbled under my breath as I walked past her.

Her next words made me jerk to a stop. "There's nothing to finish."

I somehow kept my body firmly in place as I turned my head, pinning her in place with just a look. "That's where you're wrong, baby. You don't kiss someone like that if there's nothing to finish. And don't bother denying it. I might have initiated the kiss, but you sure as fuck participated."

"Get out," she replied between clenched teeth.

I leaned in just a bit, placing a quick, unexpected kiss on her forehead. "I'll see you later, sweetheart."

Then I left before she could say anything else.

Chapter Twenty-Two

Eliza

LILLY STOOD AT the living room window, staring down at the paved ground below. "You know," she called to me, "you can't avoid him forever by locking yourself in your apartment every day."

"It's not every day," I argued as I poured myself another glass of wine. "It's only been the past three days. And in my defense, I totally felt a little flu-y when I called off work that one day."

My phone started ringing from its place on the kitchen counter for the fifth time in the past hour. The number was listed as unavailable so I hit the button on the side to silence it again. Whoever it was, I was sure they had the wrong number, but if they didn't quit calling me soon, I was two steps away from losing my shit completely.

The sound of Lilly's snort pulled my attention back to the window. "Flu-y my ass."

"Shut up," I grumbled as I grabbed my wine glass and headed to the living room. "Is he still out there?"

She glanced over her shoulder at me and the smile on her face said it all. "See for yourself."

I joined her on the other side of the window and pulled the curtains back just a bit. "Good Lord." I refused to admit to Lilly that just the sight of him sitting on the stairs outside our apartment was enough to make my belly flutter. "He's been out there all day. Why won't he just get a clue and go home already?"

"Call me crazy, but maybe because he confessed he's been in love with you for, like, *ever*, in return, you've kept yourself locked up here so you could avoid seeing him."

Ethan's head came up to the window and he lifted his hand in a wave, a small, tired smile on his face. "I wish I'd never told you about that," I muttered, dropping the curtain and stepping away. Looking at him sitting out there just hurt too much. I was living by the creed *out of sight out of mind* for as long as I could get away with it.

After Ethan left the other morning, I'd put Gary in charge while I ran back upstairs and freaked the ever-loving hell out. I'd told Lilly *everything,* and she'd spent the next three days holding it over my head.

"You know, if I didn't know any better, I'd think you were taking his side," I pouted as I threw myself back on the couch and chugged more wine.

Turning from the window, she rested her back against the wall and crossed her arms over her chest. "Good thing you know better, huh?" I rolled my eyes and took another glug as Lilly sighed and moved toward the couch. Picking my legs up, she sat on one of the cushions and rested my feet in her lap. Then she hit me with the cold, hard truth, like any best friend should, whether it was wanted or not. "Eliza, you're going to have to talk to him eventually. You know that."

"Says who?" I scoffed. "He can't stay here forever. Way I look at it, I've got a few more weeks, two months tops, before he bails back to Denver. If I can just avoid him for that time, then I'm good."

She gave me a look that said just how full of it she thought I was. "The man told you he's been in love with you since you were sixteen. He's sat outside our door the past three days when you refused to open it. You really think he's just going to give up and go home?"

"It's his usual M.O." I snapped, taking my growing anxiety out on my blameless friend.

"That's not true, and you know it. Now that the truth's out, everything's changed. You can't possibly look at him in the same light now that you know exactly what pushed him away. You've had a wall around you since you were little. The only ones you let in were your family and the few of us lucky enough to be considered a friend." I opened my mouth to argue, but she raised her hand to cut me off. "I'm not saying I blame you, babe. God, I get it. After everything your mother put you through, *I get it.* But you're an adult now. You've changed. Whether you see it in yourself or not, you're stronger now. There's no reason to keep that wall up anymore. People are going to hurt you, it's how you move past it that's going to define the type of person you are. And you aren't the type of person who doesn't forgive."

She was right. I knew she was right. However, holding on to that pain to keep people back was just so much easier than risking being hurt again. But it was also cowardly. And the last thing I wanted to be was a coward. I pulled in a deep breath and slowly let it out. "Okay," I said quietly, sitting up and putting my wine glass down on the coffee table.

"Okay?"

"Yeah. I'll go talk to him."

"That's my girl!" she cheered as I stood from the couch. "And FYI, once you two finally hook up, I want to know *all* about it. I've always been curious what he was packing in those football pants."

"Lilly!" I let out a startled laugh.

She picked up my wine glass and took a sip, "Oh, don't act all affronted, you know you've been thinking about it too."

There was no point in denying that. Just as I turned for the door, my cell began ringing again. I switched directions and moved to pick it up, groaning, "Oh my God. It's that same stupid unknown number."

"Just answer the thing and tell whoever it is they have the wrong damn number."

Finally having had enough, I slid my thumb across the screen and put it to my ear. "Look buddy. Whoever you're trying to reach isn't at this number so stop calling."

I was just about to hang up when a female voice spoke through the line. "Ms. Anderson? Eliza Anderson?"

My forehead wrinkled as I brought the phone back. "Yes? Who's this?"

"Ms. Anderson, my name is Loni Ruday. I'm a journalist with *The Inquisitor*. I'm calling about the photos that were released of you and Denver Wildcat's Ethan Prewitt. If you'd be willing to do an exclusive interview—"

"Wait, wait. What?" I interrupted as a million and

one questions bounced around in my head. "You're from a magazine? And what pictures are you talking about?"

"The ones released this morning. I'm sure you've—"

I cut her off again. "Of me and Ethan?" My eyes went to Lilly as I mouthed the word "*Google*," air-typing with my fingers just in case she didn't understand me. She jumped from the couch and went to the laptop sitting on our dining room table.

"Yes, Ms. Anderson... may I call you Eliza?"

My back went straight at her overly friendly tone. First of all, she was calling from *The Inquisitor* which was only about two steps up from a trash mag. Second, I had no freaking clue what photos she was talking about. And third, she'd been blowing my phone up for an exclusive. None of that sat well with me.

"No, you may not," I answered. "And while I'm at it, I'd prefer you not call me *at all*. I have nothing exclusive to give you or anyone else. I don't know how you got this number, but I suggest you lose it." With that, I disconnected the call and powered the phone off completely.

"Oh my God," Lilly breathed, her eyes going wide as she looked at the computer screen. Then her cheeks split into a huge grin. "This. Is. *Awesome!*"

"What? What's awesome?" I rushed over to where she was sitting and leaned over her shoulder. "Holy shit!"

Right there, big as day were pictures of me and Ethan sitting in the stands at the high school football game. The caption above read *Denver Wildcat's Ethan Prewitt getting cozy with his own personal cheerleader.*

The photos, while completely harmless, were taken to make it look like what was happening between us was much more intimate than it was. There were three pictures in total. One was of Ethan holding my hand as we walked to our seats. The next was of us sitting under the blanket, you could see his arm around my waist clear as day. And the third was snapped when he'd leaned in to whisper something in my ear. His face was half-buried in my hair and I'd just turned to look at him over my shoulder, giving the appearance we were less than a second away from kissing.

"How did they get these?" I asked as I kept scrolling.

"Hold up!" Lilly slapped my hand away from my mouse and started reading the online article out loud, picking up somewhere in the middle.

"Sources close to the couple say that things heated up between the pair when Prewitt returned home to Pembrooke, Wyoming to recuperate from surgery after a tear to his ACL took him out of the game for the rest of the season. Prewitt and the woman, now identified as longtime family friend, Eliza Anderson, reconnected since his return and have been inseparable ever since..."

"Who the hell told them that?"

"When rags like these say 'reliable source,' they mean someone who vaguely knows at least one of the parties involved in the story. But seriously, Eliza, how cool is this? I mean, look at these pictures! You two look so cute together!"

I stood tall and moved away from the chair. "Someone's spreading rumors about me and Ethan, going so far as to use my name, and all you can think about is how cute we look?"

"Well…" she trailed off, her eyes bouncing between me and the screen. "Yeah. You have to admit the coincidence with the costumes made for a perfect photo op."

"Oh my God!" I cried. "Lilly, focus! They have my *name*. That was a reporter who's been calling, which means they also *have my phone number*. You know how I am about my privacy. Hell, you just said it yourself! I hardly let anyone in! Now I'm going to have people in my business all because someone lied about me and Ethan."

Realization dawned on her face. "Oh."

"Yeah, oh." I threw my hands up and began pacing. "You know what this means? This means my privacy is shot because someone spread false rumors."

"Well…" When she trailed off, my gaze landed back on her. "Now, just hear me out," she said hesitantly. She took my silence as her chance to continue. "What if it wasn't a false rumor?"

"*What?*"

"I said hear me out!"

"Well I didn't think you were going to follow that up with something so stupid!"

She stood from her chair and came my way, placing her hands on my shoulders. "It's not stupid. He already told you he's in love with you. And before you say it, I already know damn good and well you love him too."

"I do not!"

Her lips twisted to the side in a *you're so full of shit* expression. I opened my mouth to continue to argue, only to have it slam shut. Oh my God, did I love Ethan?

I'd been so focused on the stress brought on by *him* saying it that I hadn't given myself time to sit back and think about how *I* felt.

When I was nine, going on ten, I'd convinced myself that I was going to marry him. Then he became my best friend and that love turned to something else, but it was still love, all the same. When he'd abandoned me, it had hurt worse than anything I'd ever experienced. He had broken my heart... because I loved him.

But there as a difference between loving someone and being *in* love with him. And without trust, I just... well, I just wasn't sure. All I knew for certain was that there was something substantial between us. And that's why I was so terrified.

Because the ones you loved the most were the ones with the power to truly hurt you.

"Shit," I sighed, closing my eyes and lifting a hand to rub at my forehead. "Shit, shit, shit. How did my life become such a mess?"

When I opened my eyes again, Lilly was smiling. "You need to let him in. If there's anyone who can fix this, it's him. I'm sure he's got a whole team of *people* who are paid specifically to handle stuff like this. And I bet it'll all die down before you know it."

"Yeah," I nodded, inhaling deeply and squaring my shoulders. "Yeah. He can fix this." I turned to head for the front door just seconds before someone began pounding on it. Then I heard Ethan's rugged voice call through. "Eliza, open up! There's something I need to talk to you about."

Apparently he'd just gotten the same call I had.

Chapter Twenty-Three

Ethan

Eliza was going to lose her mind.

I knew that for a fact, because I was already losing mine.

"I said to go home and recuperate, not get drunk and make an ass out of yourself in a public bar."

Apparently someone handy with a camera phone had taken pictures of my confrontation with *Kevin* at The Moose a few nights ago that didn't shine me in too good of a light. And if that wasn't bad enough, there were also pictures of me chasing Eliza out of the bar and along the sidewalk. I didn't know who had taken them, but it was guaranteed that when I found out, someone was going to pay. All of this hitting the media earlier this morning without me being aware meant I was now dealing with my pain in the ass agent when he was the last person on my mind.

"Jesus, Carl," I griped, rubbing a hand over my face. "It's not as bad as you're making it sound."

"This isn't about me making it *sound* bad. This is about how those pictures make you *look* bad. The ones of the two of you at the football game were great, don't get me wrong. People pay for that kind of publicity, and your little piece is hot, I'll give you that—"

All I saw was red. If Carl had been standing in front of me just then, I'd have probably killed him. "Talk about Eliza like that again and I swear to fucking God, I'll rip your goddamned throat out."

"Good grief," he sighed. "Calm down, would you? I was just saying—"

"Don't say shit about how she looks to me ever again and we'll be fine. Break that rule, and I break your face."

"Fuck me, she's got you whipped."

"And?" I snapped, not bothering to deny something that was one hundred percent true.

He let out another sigh. "What I'm telling you is that those original pictures were great. The ones from the bar with the caption *'Trouble Brewing between Prewitt and his Hometown Sweetheart'* are *not*."

I pulled in a breath in the effort to calm myself. The only thing Carl was worried about was how this would look in the media, while my concerns were focused on something else altogether.

"Look, Carl, it's not a big deal. It was a one time situation, that's it. There isn't going to be any more bad publicity."

"I still think we should reach out to your PR people and get ahead—"

"I don't give a shit about getting ahead of anything. What I need you to do—the *only* thing I need you to do —is find out who the fuck took those pictures and sold them to the tabloids. That's it. Job done. This shit will be old news by the end of the week."

"I hardly think—"

"Only time I pay you to think is during contract negotiations. Find me a name." With that, I hung up and took the stairs two at a time, screw my knee. I needed to contain the damage as much as humanly possible.

I knew what I said to Carl was true. My relationship status would be overlooked the minute some tween pop princess flashed her vag for all the world to see, or some douchebag singer lost his shit and walked off stage at a packed concert. That wasn't what worried me. What worried me was how Eliza was going to handle it.

Part of having that wall up around herself was keeping her personal life personal. She was an extremely private person. The only ones who got the real Eliza were those of us in her inner circle. And even then, it was only bits and pieces. Most of the time, I felt like I was the only one that got *all* of her. Her father and Chloe got her love, that was certain, but she didn't talk to them about the scars her mom left behind. That was only for me.

"Eliza, open up!" I shouted, knocking on the door a little harder than necessary. "There's something I need to talk to you about." To my surprise, the door swung open less than a second later and just seeing Eliza standing there before me in a pair of yoga pants and a thread bare, well-worn hoodie made my heart stutter. "Baby—"

"The internet knows my name."

My head jerked back and my eyebrows dipped in confusion. "What?"

"The internet knows my name. And they think we're a couple."

Well, that explained her bizarre declaration. I held my hands up in a placating gesture, "I know, sweetheart. And I swear to God, I'm already taking care of it. I talked to my agent and told him I wanted the name of the person who'd taken those pictures at The Moose"

"The Moose?" she cut me off. It was obviously her turn to be confused. "What are you talking about?"

And *fuck*. "Wait... what are *you* talking about?"

"I'm talking about the pictures online of us at the football game."

"Ah. Okay. Well..." I paused, trying to think of a delicate way to inform her that those weren't the only photos about us online. Before I had a chance to lay it out gently, Lilly was there, clutching the laptop to her chest.

"Holy crap! Look at this." She spun the screen around for Eliza to see. "Whoever took those pictures at the game must have taken these from the bar the other night too."

I watched with growing panic as her eyes went wide. She studied the screen for what felt like an eternity before looking back at me. Her lips parted to speak, but I jumped in first, not wanting to risk her slamming the door in my face.

"I'm going to fix it."

Eliza's mouth snapped shut. Then opened again. Then closed. Then, "Really?"

"Absolutely," I answered vehemently. "I've already talked to my agent. He's going to hunt down the name of the person who sold those photos. I'll get them pulled down. And I know you hate any invasions of your privacy, but I swear this will die down. Trust me, I've dealt with shit like this before. Football players are small time."

She bit her lip, looking hesitant to believe me.

"He's right. You know how much I love those gossip mags. As soon as a rapper cheats on his more-famous-than-him wife with their housekeeper, which happens like, *all the time*, people will forget all about this." Lilly chirped, and I made a mental note to stuff her Christmas stocking with twenty dollar bills.

Eliza's eyes bounced back and forth between the two of us before she finally released what appeared to be a relieved breath. "All right. If you say you're going to handle it, I trust you."

Those last three words hit me right in the fucking chest, stealing the air from my lungs. I didn't realize until that very moment that I hadn't been waiting weeks to hear her say she trusted me... I'd been waiting six goddamned years. I knew it wasn't her full trust that I'd earned, but just that little bit was enough to make me feel invincible.

"Good," I declared, pushing my way into the apartment past two suddenly bewildered looking ladies. "Now that that's out of the way and you're finally *answering the door*, I've decided I'm taking you to dinner."

"I'm sorry..." Eliza blinked a few times. "What?"

"Dinner. A date. I know you get the concept of a

date." I narrowed my eyes at her. "Seeing as you went on one with *the wrong guy* not all that long ago."

"Ethan," Eliza sighed, reaching up to rub her forehead as Lilly shoved the front door closed with a huge smile on her face.

"What a great idea!"

At her friend's declaration, Eliza's head shot up. She glared at Lilly at the same time I smiled... *huge*, having just discovered I had another person fighting in my corner when it came to winning Eliza.

"No it's not," Eliza grumbled, looking from me, back to her roommate. "Have you forgotten about the fact that there's someone out there following us around and snapping pictures?" I couldn't help but think she looked fucking adorable when she was throwing attitude.

"Then you guys can stay in," Lilly replied, causing me to frown because having her along as a third wheel on our date wasn't the best solution to me. I was just about to mention that when she continued talking. "And the timing couldn't be more perfect. It just so happened that I planned on spending the night with my parents tonight anyway. What a happy coincidence!" She clapped her hands and smiled in a way that read loud and clear it wasn't a coincidence at all. And I suspected her parents were going to be in for a surprise when she showed up at their door.

Eliza's sigh told me she was about to argue so I jumped on Lilly's train of thought. "I'll make you dinner," I announced, surprising both women into speechlessness.

"You cook?" Eliza asked.

"Yep," I answered with a confidence I most certainly wasn't feeling. I didn't know a thing about cooking. If I were being honest, I didn't know jack shit about cooking, but I couldn't possibly be any worse than my sister. It was Pembrooke lore that Harlow Murphy was one of the worst cooks to ever walk the planet. I was sure I could figure it out. How hard could it be? "You're not thrilled with the idea of going out in public just yet, and you spend every day cooking for others. Tonight I'll cook for you."

I watched in amazement as the uncertainty on her face shifted just slightly and her expression grew warm and soft. She liked the idea of someone else taking care of her, and I fucking *loved* that.

"Brilliant!" Lilly clapped. "All right kiddos, I'm going to pack a bag and get out of your hair. Don't burn the house down while I'm gone, say no to drugs, and all the cool kids practice safe sex." With that, she flounced down the hall into her bedroom, only to reappear about a minute later with an overnight bag on her shoulder. She gave a still stunned Eliza a loud, smacking kiss on the cheek and announced, "Love ya!" Then she gave me a menacing double finger point before disappearing out the front door.

"She's terrifying," I said once she was gone.

"She can be, but most of the time she's just really freaking annoying."

"I don't know," I laughed, turning to look at Eliza, "I kind of like her."

She glared, which only made me want to grab her and kiss her... and much, *much* more. "You would."

Closing the space between us, I did one of the many things I'd been dying to do since that morning in her kitchen. I slid my fingers into her thick, soft, dark hair and lowered my face close to hers. Her breathing instantly went erratic at my touch and her cheeks grew flushed.

"Don't act like that kiss didn't affect you," I whispered softly, my lips only centimeters away from hers. "I knew you felt it just as much as I did the minute your body melted into mine."

"I—" I could tell she was just about to object, but something flashed in the hazel eyes and what came out of her mouth was unexpected. "There's nothing in the apartment to eat."

"What?" My head cocked to the side in confusion.

"There's no food. Lilly and I kind of suck at grocery

shopping. There's nothing to cook, and there's no more wine left. And I haven't even had a shower today!"

I couldn't hold in my laughter at her flustered rush of words. She was grasping at any excuse she could possibly think of. Leaning in, I gave her a quick peck on the lips and stated, "Go take a shower, baby. I'll head down to Mabel's and pick some stuff up."

"But—"

I silenced her with another kiss, this one just a few seconds longer, but it was still long enough to make her eyes a little glassy when I pulled back. "Shower. I'll take care of it."

"Okay," she whispered, sounding somewhat drugged. She turned and started down the hallway, and I waited, watching her insanely sexy ass sway in those yoga pants. The spell was broken when I heard the sound of the bathroom door shutting firmly.

I shook away the dirty thoughts filling my head and tried to get my growing erection under control as I moved in the direction of the front door. I had groceries to buy and a dinner to make.

And somewhere in between those two, I hoped like hell that I'd figure out the art of cooking.

Chapter Twenty-Four

Ethan

IT WASN'T UNTIL I got to Mabel's Corner Market and began scanning the aisles that I started to feel anxiety knot in my stomach. That hope I'd been holding on to that inspiration would strike when I got there was nowhere to be found.

"Fuck me," I grunted, running my hands over my face. It was when I'd finally dropped my hands and the items in front of me lit up like a beacon, that inspiration finally struck. "Genius!" I hissed to myself as I grabbed the items and tossed them in the basket. I ran around the rest of the store like a mad man and got everything else I needed to make Eliza dinner.

Just as I started for the register, something out of the corner of my eye caught my attention, stopping me in my tracks. I probably stood there for a good three minutes contemplating if I should toss them in the basket or not, and finally decided better safe than sorry. I didn't have to tell Eliza I'd purchased the condoms. I wasn't making assumptions about where the night might lead. But if things went in that direction naturally— Christ, please let them head in that direction—I'd kick my own ass if we had to stop because neither of us had any protection.

I wasn't even going to *consider* what I'd do if she just so happened to have condoms of her own. My head would probably explode. Better off to just grab my own box if we went down that road.

"Well hey there, football star," Mabel crooned, smiling that creepy smile at me.

"Hey there, Mabel."

"Saw about you and that sweet Eliza on the inter-web." She winked, and good God, that wink made me shiver... not in a good way. "So is it true? Are you offi-cially off the market and cozying up with the Sherriff's daughter?"

I didn't hesitate in my answer. "Yep. We're togeth-er." I just left out the part where Eliza wasn't totally onboard just yet. I had complete faith that I could get her there. And I was hoping sooner than later, because I was running out of patience.

"So you're grocery shopping for your new girl?

That's so cute." She smiled as I slid my basket across the countertop for her to start scanning.

"Thanks," I grinned, feeling a new boost of confidence, "I'm making her dinner tonight."

At my admission, Mabel froze in the middle of emptying the basket. "You're kidding right?" she asked, her weathered skin wrinkling even more as she curled her lip at me.

"What?"

Her gaze bounced from the items she'd emptied from the basket back to me. Her look screamed loud and clear that she thought I was an idiot.

"Grilled cheese sandwiches and tomato soup are football season staples!" I argued.

"You're gonna feed a professional cook, a woman who went to culinary school, tomato-flavored paste in a can and white bread with melted, processed cheese." It wasn't a question, and if I was reading between the lines correctly, what she actually meant was *'Have you lost your fucking mind?'*. But I didn't really have much of a choice.

"Look, I've never cooked before, but I figured I couldn't really screw up soup and a hot sandwich. It's the best I could do on a time crunch, okay?" I didn't know why I was defending myself to the woman, it's not like her opinion really mattered in the long run, but as she stared me down—obviously finding me lacking—I just couldn't help myself.

"Mmhmm." Her hum was chalk-full of distaste. "Well, let's just hope you're better at it than your sister. And I'm fairly certain you won't be needing *these*," she held up the box of condoms. "Not with what you've got planned for dinner."

"Just ring everything up," I ground out between my clenched teeth, thinking to myself that, never again would I engage Mabel in conversation. It never went well for me.

ELIZA

OH GOD.

Ohgodohgodohgod.

What had I gotten myself into? I was standing in my bathroom, wrapped in nothing but a towel as water dripped from my hair onto my shoulders, losing my mind because I'd agreed to a *date* with *Ethan Prewitt.*

And what scared me the most was that I was actually *excited.* The thought of him in my kitchen, making me dinner because he wanted to take care of me had a swarm of butterflies fluttering around in my belly. I felt that guard I kept up around him lowering, and no matter what I did to keep it in place, the damn thing just wouldn't work.

He said he loved me. Somewhere deep, *deep* down I believed him. It was just that giving him my full trust again was harder than putting my heart in his hands. Because if I were being honest with myself, he already had my heart. Always had.

That was part of the problem. Ever since my mother abandoned me, giving someone else the power to hurt me that way was something I'd always shied away from. I'd let Ethan in once before and look what had happened. Would allowing him in a second time really be smart?

And what would happen once he went back to Denver.

There were so many questions swirling around in my head, questions I couldn't figure out the answers to, that I couldn't think straight.

But despite all the questions, all the doubt, one thing was standing out in my mind the most. I *wanted* to give this a shot. I *wanted* to believe him. And most of all, I *wanted* to see where this would go, if I were strong enough to survive whatever was to happen.

With a frustrated sigh, I swiped the fog off the bathroom mirror and stared at my reflection.

"You can do this," I whispered to myself. "You're a strong, independent woman. It's just a date." I pulled in a breath and closed my eyes for several seconds. "Just a date with a really, *really* gorgeous guy that you've loved pretty much your whole life that's hurt you once already."

Shit, I really sucked at this pep-talk stuff.

I gave myself a whole body shake and looked back in the mirror. "You've got this. You've got this. You've—"

I ended on a small shriek when my cellphone on the bathroom counter began to ring, startling me from my monologue.

"Hello?" I answered without looking at the screen, holding a hand to my chest in an effort to calm my erratic heart.

"You're in *trooooooouble.*"

I pulled the phone away from my ear and looked to see who the caller was. "Chloe? What are you talking about? Why am I in trouble?"

"Your father is going to *flip* when he sees those pictures that are floating all around the internet of you and Ethan."

"Shit," I hissed out a breath, propping one hand on the counter to hold myself up. "Has he seen them yet?"

"Not yet, seeing as he's all man and doesn't peruse trashy magazines online on a regular basis. Is it true?"

"Is what true?"

"You and Ethan," she shouted through the line. "They're saying you're a couple. Is it true? I mean, I saw the pictures. You two look quite cozy."

"Oh my God, Chloe," I whisper yelled, not wanting Ethan to overhear in case he'd already made it back from the store. "You were there the night of the football game. You know those pictures were taken out of context."

"So... it's not true then?" she asked, sounding somewhat defeated. Damn it, how had this become my life? I actually missed the boring days where I went to work, came home, drank wine, and went to bed.

"No... yes... Ugh! I don't... I don't know, okay. I'm a little confused right now."

She remained silent for several seconds. "Well what does *that* mean?"

I turned and rested my butt on the counter, using my free hand to massage my forehead. "Things are... a little complicated right now." I blew out a breath and admitted, "Ethan's making me dinner tonight. It's kind of a date."

"*Kind* of a date?" she asked incredulously. "How is something *kind* of a date? I swear to God, I don't understand young people these days."

I let out a small laugh. "Okay, so it *is* a date, all right? Happy now?"

"Extremely," she answered exuberantly. "But you're going to need to tell your father before he finds out from someone in town. You know how he gets. How a man as hotheaded as he is was ever granted access to firearms is beyond me, I swear. He's not going to like that Ethan didn't come to him first."

My back straightened and I was suddenly overwhelmed with the desire to defend Ethan. "Well he'll just have to get over it. I'm not a little girl anymore, Chlo. I'm twenty-two."

"*I* know that, sweetheart. And *you* know that. But when, in all your life, have you known your father to be rational when it comes to his girls?"

"I just..." God, I couldn't handle any more stress. "I need you to cover for me for a little while longer, okay? I just need to get my head around this before I talk to Daddy..." I trailed off before giving her the honest truth. "I'm scared," I said in a quiet voice. "I'm scared, and I have no clue what I'm doing. I just need a little more time."

"Okay, honey," she answered softly, giving me the sweet, nurturing Chloe I needed just then. "I've got your back, you know that. I always will. But let me just say this... sometimes the things that scare us the most are the things that turn out to mean *everything*. You open yourself up to what's happening between you and Ethan, and I have a feeling you'll get the kind of happy you've always deserved, but never allowed yourself to have."

I wasn't quite sure I believed in what she was saying as much as she did, but that ball of tension that had been coiling in my chest began to loosen ever so slightly. I opened my mouth to thank her when a sudden loud, piercing screech filled the air all around me.

"Shit! Chloe, I have to go."

"What's happening?"

"I'm not sure, but I have an idea." Boy, did I have an idea. Ethan *was* Harlow's brother, after all. "I'll call you later, promise. Love you."

"Love you too."

Rushing from the bathroom to the bedroom, I dropped my towel and snatched on a pair or loose, cotton sweats and a tank before taking back off in the direction of the kitchen. Because a Prewitt and smoke detectors did not bode well.

Chapter Twenty-Five

Eliza

C OMING TO A grinding halt at the sight in front of me, I couldn't do anything other than slap my hands over my mouth and stare, wide-eyed, as I tried my best to suppress my laughter.

"Son of a fucking bitch, mother of sweet Hell," Ethan growled as he stood on a chair in the middle of the kitchen, one of my floral patterned hand towels in his hands as he waved it frantically back and forth in front of the smoke detector. The kitchen and living room were steadily filling with smoke as Ethan continued to curse and fan the still chirping detector.

Finally losing the war against my laughter, I dropped my hands and began giggling hysterically. His gaze shot to mine. "Open the door and windows!"

I spun on my bare feet and ran to the front door, jerking in wide open before moving to the living room window to do the same. Once finished with that, I rushed back into the kitchen, skirting Ethan where he stood on the chair... *still* waving the towel, and twisted the nobs to the burners, turning them off. I grabbed the now ruined skillet and pot and tossed them both into the sink. I turned the water on and let it cool the scorched metal with a loud hiss as the smoke finally began to clear from the room and the loud screeching thankfully stopped.

Ethan slowly climbed down from the chair, put it back at the dining room table and made his way to where I stood by the sink. "You destroyed my Emeril Lagasse cookware," I said in a choked voice, trying not to burst into another fit of laughter as I picked up the skillet and studied the charred-beyond-recognition food that seemed to be permanently bonded to the bottom. I wasn't exactly sure what I was looking at, but at first glance it looked like a brick of tar.

I felt his breath on the back of my neck as he said, "I'll buy you more."

His low, gravelly voice danced up my spine, sending a shiver through my body. I dropped the skillet and picked up the pot. I couldn't even begin to guess what had been in there. "What were you cooking? Or *trying* to cook?" My giggle turned into a yelp when Ethan's hands came to my waist and he began to tickle.

"Grilled cheese sandwiches and tomato soup," he answered once he was finished with his tickle torture.

I couldn't have stopped my face from curling in disgust if I wanted to... which I really didn't, because *eww*.

"It's a football season staple!" he shouted at the ceiling before finally looking back down at me. "Okay... so I might have over exaggerated my skills in the kitchen."

I couldn't stop the smile that spread across my face. He just looked so cute and disheveled. "Exaggerated by how much?" I asked, having a feeling I already knew the answer, but wanting to make him sweat a little more just for the fun of it.

Reaching up, he scratched at the back of his neck uncomfortably before stating, "In the sense that I've never cooked anything before."

Those walls around me just kept getting lower and lower. But at that very moment, I felt way too good to stress about it. I felt light, carefree. Standing in my smoky apartment with my ruined cookware, I actually felt... happy.

"Come on," I said, grabbing Ethan's hand and

pulling him toward the door that lead to the interior stairs.

His fingers tightened around mine as he asked, "Where are we going?"

"To my *real* kitchen. It's time for your first cooking lesson."

We walked down the stairs in silence, Ethan's hand gripping mine tightly as I lead him down the hall and through the door that led into the kitchen of Sinful Sweets Café. The restaurant was closed for the night so we had the whole place to ourselves, and as I flipped the switches, turning on the lights, I released a deep breath, feeling at peace, at home in the place of my dreams. For me, there was nothing better than cooking...

Or at least that's how I felt before Ethan came back into my life.

I had to tug my hand twice to get him to let it go, but once he did I walked over to the shelf and pulled two, freshly laundered and folded aprons down, tossing one to him. "Put this on. You're going to cook in a legit kitchen, you have to dress the part."

With a sexy smirk that did crazy things to my insides, Ethan doubled wrapped the strings of the apron around his waist and tied it off in the front. I did the same as I headed for the walk-in to start pulling out everything I needed.

"So what are we making?" he asked as I moved past him and over to the prep counter, where I dropped all my ingredients.

"I'm going to start off easy on you—"

"Thank fuck," he muttered under his breath, causing me to laugh again. My laughter instantly died when, in two quick steps, he was directly in front of me, his hand coming up to rest against my cheek as his thumb dragged gently across my lower lip. "I love it when you laugh," he said softly. "So beautiful all the time, but when you laugh..." He gave his head a small shake. "Fucking gorgeous. Most beautiful girl I've ever laid eyes on."

My body shivered at his declaration, and I found myself swaying closer to him as if my body had a mind of its own. I cleared my throat and tried to shake the sudden cloudiness taking over my head at Ethan's close proximity.

"Um... okay. I'm going to teach you to make spaghetti," I tried to speak confidently. "You'll be surprised at how easy it is. Just... do everything I tell you... and maybe stay away from the stove unless I'm right next to you," I teased, earning myself another one of his killer smirks. Good Lord, I was in trouble.

I spent the next hour—between all the teasing and laughing—teaching Ethan everything he needed to know about making spaghetti. He chopped the herbs to add to the sauce, he sautéed garlic, I even taught him how to make homemade meatballs. Surprisingly enough, he was a pretty fast learner, picking up everything I was telling him with ease. It was the most fun I could remember having in years, and it was almost like Ethan and I had slid seamlessly back into the friendship we used to have... *almost*. Because that charged undercurrent that kept crackling through the air every time we touched most certainly hadn't been there back when we were kids. That was something altogether new, and I would have been lying if I said it didn't add an element of excitement. It was thrilling, almost like we were doing something we shouldn't and were at risk of getting caught. And as the evening pressed on, I found I struggled to keep my eyes off of him.

The meatballs were ready, the sauce simmering on the stove when I told him, "Okay. You did it! All that's left to do is strain the pasta, and we'll be set."

I stood back and watched as he carried the pot over to the sink and dumped the contents into the colander I'd put down for him. The way his biceps bulged as he lifted the heavy pot made his t-shirt pull across his broad chest and back. His muscles rippled and flexed in a hypnotizing manner as he poured, and with his attention momentarily diverted, I was able to stare at his perfect ass in his faded jeans. I'd never considered a man to be beautiful before. I'd seen rugged, handsome, hot, but those words didn't properly describe Ethan. He encompassed all of that and so much more. He truly was beautiful.

He turned from the sink, and by the knowing grin on his handsome face, I knew I hadn't diverted my gaze in enough time. He knew I'd just been checking him out. Ignoring the low, rumbling chuckle he released, I pulled some plates down for us. We piled our dishes high with food and I went and grabbed a bottle of red wine and two glasses from the bar to drink with our meal. We sat on stools pulled close to the counter and dug in.

As soon as the first bite hit my mouth, I let out a moan, the slight tang of the tomatoes wasn't overpowered by the garlic and basil in the slightest. It was fabulous. "Ethan, this is really good," I said through a mouthful of food. "Definitely an A plus worthy meal."

I swallowed and lifted my wineglass to take a sip. He remained silent, and when I placed my glass back on the metal counter to meet his gaze, what I saw staring back at me made my chest tighten.

"Glad you approve, baby." His voice was ten times rougher than normal and the lust glinting in his eyes had darkened the unusual color substantially. "But I'm going to need you to stop making sounds like that."

I had no clue what came over me just then, but with

the way we'd been dancing around each other all night, and how my body felt like a live wire every time he touched me, I just couldn't help myself, I pushed. My mouth opened and the words came out with no thought.

"Or what?"

I could have sworn I heard him growl as he pushed his plate aside and leaned in closer to me. "Or I'll be forced to lay you out on this counter and fuck you until my name is the only goddamned word you're able to say."

My thighs clenched reflexively at the rush of desire that suddenly waved over me. My breathing picked up and some part of me, a part I'd never experienced, was unleashed. Gone was hesitant, guarded Eliza. In her place was a daring woman who wanted every single thing Ethan had just spelled out.

It was like an out of body experience. Leaning closer, I swiped my finger through the remaining tomato sauce on my plate and closed my eyes. The moan was much lower and much longer the second time around, and when I opened my eyes to meet his, I knew mine were full of challenge.

And in that moment I didn't want anything more than for him to accept that challenge.

His chest rose and fell manically as he reached up

and grabbed my face between his hands. "This happens there's no going back. You understand me?"

Unable to form words, I nodded.

That must not have been good enough for him, because he continued with his warning. "Once I feel what it's like to be inside you, that's it. You're mine. No more fucking around. No more games. It's me and you. You sure you want that, baby?"

"Yes," I moaned, wanting nothing else in the world more than that.

"You're going to be mine? No more fighting? No more pushing me away?"

I nodded again, my brain so clouded with lust I wasn't fully absorbing what he was saying, but I would have promised anything at that moment for just a taste of him. "Yours, Ethan."

His lips came so close, they brushed against mine as he said, "Then tell me what you want, baby. Tell me and I'll give it to you. I'll give you fucking everything."

Reaching up to rest my hands on his strong chest, I opened my mouth and told him exactly what I wanted.

"Fuck me, Ethan."

Chapter Twenty-Six

Ethan

WITH ONE SWEEP of my arm the dishes on the counter went flying to the floor, shattering into pieces, but both of us were too consumed in each other to care. Grasping Eliza by her hips, I pulled her from the stool she was sitting on, pinning her hot body against mine as I went for her mouth in a brutal, punishing kiss.

She met the kiss with the same exact intensity, nipping and biting and thrusting her tongue against mine in a passionate battle for dominance. My hands left her hips just long enough for my fingers to slide into the waistband of her sweat pants and rip them and her panties down her thighs. She stepped out and kicked them away without removing her lips from mine.

My hands glided over her bare ass and a deep,

throaty moan rumbled up from her chest and down into mine, causing my fingers to clench against her warm, soft skin. "Oh, God," she whimpered against my mouth, spurring me into action. With my hands already in place, I lifted her up and set her down on the countertop. "Off," she panted, disengaging just long enough to pull at my shirt in a desperate attempt to get it over my head. "Take this off."

Reaching behind my head, I grabbed the collar of my tee and ripped it off, dropping it on the floor by her pants. I moved in for another kiss when her hands came up to my chest and halted my progress. Instead, her lips and tongue slid across the flesh of my pecs. Her teeth bit down on my nipple just hard enough to elicit a groan from me. "God, you're beautiful," she muttered against my heated skin as she moved up and bit at my collarbone, leaving a scorching path in her wake.

My hands moved down and hooked into the hem of her shirt. The second I began to pull it up, her hands and mouth came off me. She lifted her arms to help guide my movement. "Jesus," I breathed once I had the shirt off. She hadn't been wearing a bra beneath her tank. Anything my mind had conjured up about Eliza's body paled in comparison to the real thing. She was perfect. Absolutely, unequivocally perfect. And the need to taste her everywhere rushed over me like a tidal wave.

"God, Ethan," she moaned, her fingers sliding into my hair when I lifted her breast on my hand and sucked the dusty pink nipple into my mouth. Her skin tasted even better than I could have imagined. I couldn't get enough. I sucked and pulled at her nipples until they formed tight, hard peaks. By the time I moved away from them, sliding my way down her body, she was a writhing, panting mess. Her hips circling frantically as she begged, "Please. God, please don't stop."

"Not stopping," I told her in a rough, hungry voice. "But I need to taste you, baby. I've been dying to put my mouth on you."

Placing a palm in the center of her stomach, I gave her a gentle push, moving her backward to just where I needed her. Eliza's head fell back on a desperate cry as her hands went behind her on the countertop to hold her up. "Christ. I've loved you for so long. I've been dreaming of this since I ran into you at Mabel's," I growled against her belly as my hand skated down her trembling skin to the juncture between her thighs. "Never stopped thinking about you," I said softly as my fingers trailed through her folds, feeling just how wet she was for me. "Not once in six goddamned years, baby."

"Ethan, please," she said on a pained whisper, needing me to touch her just as badly as I needed to.

Wanting to give her everything she craved, I pushed

two fingers into her tight, drenched heat, reveling in the gasp she let out as her back arched. Unable to wait another second, I bent down and put my mouth right where I'd wanted to be for so long. The instant Eliza's taste flooded my mouth I was lost, crazed with desire to claim every inch of her as my own.

My fingers plunged in and out of her as my tongue circled her clit over and over. I felt her getting tighter. That, coupled with the way her fingers were suddenly yanking at my hair, told me she was close. I wanted to feel her lose control. I wanted to feel that release against my mouth. Knowing just what she needed to go over the edge, I shoved my fingers in and curled them up at the same time I sucked her clit between my lips.

That did it. Eliza's entire body locked up as her climax overtook her. "*Ethan*," she shouted as she pulsed against my lips. Her sweet, musky flavor was like ambrosia, and I knew there was no way I'd ever get enough of all things Eliza. She was branded beneath my skin.

I stayed with her, petting and licking softly as the last of her orgasm seeped out of her, until her upper body gave out and she collapsed back against the counter, unable to stay sitting any longer.

I stood tall and reached into my back pocket, pulling out my wallet. Thank Christ I'd been of sound mind enough to put one of those condoms in my wallet while she'd been in the shower.

"Sit up," I ground out, drunk on lust. I yanked the condom out and tossed the wallet aside, dropping the foil packet beside her thigh as my hands moved to the button of my jeans.

Just as I'd demanded, Eliza sat up, still breathing heavy, and once she saw what I was doing, her fingers went into action, pushing mine out of the way as she ripped at the button fly, popping them open in quick succession. Her head tilted up, her lips puckered just slightly in a silent request that I was all too happy to oblige. I moved back in for a kiss and her tiny hands slid around my waist and down, pushing at my jeans. Her nails dug into my ass as the kiss grew more heated.

"Ethan, please," she begged.

"Tell me," I replied, pulling her bottom lip between my teeth. "Tell me what you want, and I'll give it to you."

"Need you," she gasped, pulling away just far enough to free my straining cock the rest of the way. "Need you now."

Snatching up the condom, I ripped it opened with my teeth and slid it on in record time. My hands went behind her knees and jerked her ass to the edge of the counter, but, as much as it killed me, I didn't push into her. "You mine?" I asked, taking my erection in my hand and sliding the head of my cock through her folds.

She nodded and wriggled, trying to force me into her.

I circled her clit, still refusing to give her exactly what she was craving. Not until I heard the words I needed. "Say it."

"Stop playing games," she panted, dragging her nails across my waist from back to front. Her hazel eyes were completely glassed over, and just knowing I was the one that made her look like that, who drove her out of her mind, made my chest expand.

"No games, baby. Need to hear it from your beautiful lips." I pushed in, just an inch, but even that was enough to almost make me lose control...*almost*. "Please, sweetheart," I whispered. I'd never begged for anything in my life, never had anything so important it was worth begging for. But for Eliza I'd drop to my goddamned knees and bleed myself dry at her feet. "I need the words."

"I'm yours."

With that, I plunged in to the hilt.

"*ETHAN!*" Her head snapped back and her hands came to my shoulders, holding on tight.

"Look at me," I growled, pulling out and driving back in as one of my hands dove into her hair. I fisted it and used that to pull her head back up. I wanted her gaze on mine while I fucked her. "Fuck, *fuck!*" I grunted as I thrust into her like a mad man. "Feel so good, Eliza. *Christ*, you were made for me, baby. You're mine."

"I'm yours," she answered as her hands slid from my shoulders into the hair at the base of my neck. "Harder, Ethan."

With one hand already in her hair, I wrapped my other arm around her waist and pulled her chest flush against mine, loving the feel of her naked breasts against me as I gave her what she asked for, fucking her harder.

"Always, mine," I said as I buried myself deep and circled my hips, grinding into her clit, causing her to moan into my mouth.

"Always. *Faster.*"

I drove harder, faster, to the point where I would have feared I was hurting her had her walls not been clutching around my dick like a vice. She was just seconds from going off like I rocket, and I couldn't think of anything better than feeling Eliza come all over me. "Been mine your whole life." My next words were punctuated by the snap of my hips. "Always. Will. Be."

With that, she clamped down around me so hard it almost hurt as I swallowed down her screams of release. She came for what felt like an eternity, so hard a tear slipped passed her eyelid and trailed down her cheek. It was too much. Being inside her, feeling her core holding tight, I couldn't stop myself from coming right along with her. I thrust once, twice, three times before driving in and exploding, letting her pussy milk me dry, demanding everything inside of me, draining me completely dry. Fuck, fuck, *fuck!* "Oh, Christ, *Eliza!* I'm coming!" I buried my face in her neck as an orgasm so strong I thought I'd pass the hell out washed through my entire body.

In the back of my mind, I heard her cry out again, felt her tighten up around me, and I knew my own climax had spurred yet another one for her. I don't know how long I stood there, my entire body trembling thanks to the best sex I'd ever had in my life, but it wasn't until Eliza's hands started gliding up and down my back in a soothing gesture, that I was able to find the strength to pull my head from her neck.

"That was..." she trailed off on a sigh as one of her hands came up to push my hair off my damp forehead before resting against my cheek.

"Yeah," I answered, pressing closer into her touch.

Her eyes cleared and focused as her gorgeous face lit with a smile. "You broke my dishes. What is it with you and kitchenware?"

With a chuckle, I released her hair and circled both of my arms around her, loving how it felt to just hold her.

"I'll buy you more. Anything you want or need. I'll give it to you." I pressed a quick kiss to her lips before pulling back and finishing, "For the rest of your life, baby."

Something unsettling flickered across her face, causing my arms to squeeze. "Don't shut down on me," I demanded, knowing exactly what that look meant. "Not now. Not again.

"Ethan," she sighed, dropping her hand from my face. I immediately missed its warmth.

"No," I snapped.

Her eyelids lowered into slits. "You don't even know what I was going to say. You won't even let me speak."

"I don't need to hear it to know what you're going to say. And I'm not letting you go there. Especially when I'm still fucking inside you."

"Just listen—"

"No." At my clipped word, she let out an agitated huff. "Whatever you're about to say is bullshit."

Her back stiffened and her palms came to my chest to try and push me away, but I wasn't moving. I wasn't ready to lose our connection. "That's not fair!"

"You need to listen to me right now, and get what I'm telling you. I'm. Not. Letting. Go. Understand?" I proved my point with another squeeze. "I'm in love with you. I lost you for six years and those have been the most miserable years of my life. I've finally got you back, and

I'll be damned if I let you slip through my fingers again. I'll do whatever I have to do prove that you're safe with me. Please, *Christ*, Eliza. Just..." I sucked in a much-needed breath in an attempt to calm the aching pressure suddenly building in my chest. "Please, just let me show you. I can't lose you again. I can't *lose you*," I finished, my voice sounding completely ravaged, even to my own ears.

"Okay, okay," she said quickly, cupping both my cheeks in her hands. "I'm here, Ethan. I'm right here... okay?" Dropping my forehead to hers, I let out an unsteady breath. "I'm right here," she repeated.

"Thank you," I whispered as the last of the pain in my chest eased.

"Come on," she said, lifting my face and placing a kiss on each of my eyelids before moving to my lips. "Let's go upstairs." I watched as the concern that had been marring her brow quickly melted away and she smiled. "My mattress is *much* more comfortable than this counter."

We both laughed as I pulled her in for a hug before finally breaking our connection. She wanted to take me to her bed, I was totally fine with that.

She didn't have to tell me twice.

Chapter Twenty-Seven

Eliza

I WOKE UP feeling slightly confused at the tight, persistent throbbing between my thighs. My eyes slowly peeled open, blinking against the rays of sunlight peeking through the curtains of my bedroom window. It took me a few seconds to clear the sleep from my brain, but as soon as I did, I knew the source of the throb.

"Morning," Ethan's raspy morning voice rumbled in my ear before his mouth returned to the bare skin of my shoulder.

The arm beneath me twisted, his hand palming my breast as the other rested on my thigh, his fingertips tracing a random pattern on my flesh close to my center. But the thing I noticed the most was the thick, hard length of his erection digging against my ass as his hips pressed tighter against me.

"How'd you sleep, sweetheart?"

"Mmm," I moaned in response, closing my eyes as I dropped my head back against his shoulder. "Like a baby. You?"

"Best sleep I've had in my life. But waking up was even better."

"*Yes*," I hissed as he lifted my left leg up and pulled it over his hip, opening me up for him to continue to play.

"You love it when I touch you," he growled, biting at the sensitive place where my neck met my shoulder before soothing the sting with his tongue. "You're so goddamned wet for me." I moaned again, incapable of speech as he toyed with my body in the most delicious way. "You want me to make you come, Eliza?"

"God, yes." And I did. I felt like I'd tear apart if he didn't let me come, which was amazing considering I'd lost count of the number of orgasms he'd given me the night before. "Please, Ethan." As soon as those two words escaped my mouth his heat disappeared from my back. "No!"

I twisted my head and began to turn, only to have his large hands hold me in place as he moved back against me a second later. "Relax, baby. I'm not leaving you." My chest tightened and my heart flipped at those four little words. *I'm not leaving you.* God, how I wished those words meant something altogether different at that very moment, but before I could lose myself to the melancholy, the sound of a condom wrapper being opened tore through the room. Ethan hooked my thigh around his once more and pressed in, blanking my mind to anything and everything that didn't have to do with how he felt inside of me.

Last night had been fast, hungry, a desperate joining of two people who craved each other, but this was something completely different.

Ethan's strokes were slower, methodical, yet no less potent. He was taking his time building me up toward that glorious finale, and while his touches and kisses were more gentle, the release I felt brewing promised to be no less intense than all the others he'd given me in our short time together.

"Kiss me," he said against my neck.

Unable to deny him anything he wanted, I tilted my head back and twisted, giving him perfect access to my mouth as his thrust began to speed up. "You feel so amazing," I whispered against his lips, completely lost to the sensation of what he was doing to me. "I love having you inside me."

His hand at my breast tightened, his other arm wrapping around me to pull me closer. "I just love you."

His response made me pull in a surprised breath. No matter how many times he'd said it, I never grew more used to hearing those words come out of his mouth. "Ethan—" I started, unsure of what exactly I was going to say, but he silenced me with another kiss.

The arm around my waist loosened and his hand slid down to where we were joined together. His fingers worked magic as he continued to thrust, and within seconds I was spiraling down, crying out his name as starbursts exploded against the backs of my eyelids.

"*Eliza*," he groaned, burying himself as deep as he could go, his face in my hair, and his arms holding me tight as he rode out his own climax.

After a few seconds, once we both caught our breaths he lifted his head and gave me a peck on the lips before gracing me with his brilliant smile. "Now that's the kind of wakeup I'm looking forward to." Before I could respond, he pulled out and climbed from the bed, grabbing my ankle and yanking me across the mattress. "Come on, baby. I want to shower with you before you have to get to work.

I followed behind him in a fog, feeling like I'd just woken up in a twilight zone.

When had my life become so complicated?

"They've doubled in numbers." I turned at the sound of my waitress Megan's voice. "And one of them even tried to come in and sit down like he was going to order something, but when Becky got to his table all he asked about was you and Ethan, so she told him to get his hairy ass out, we didn't need his money."

"Did he listen?" Chloe asked from the other side of the kitchen where she was working with her pastry team.

Megan giggled. "Not at first, but when she held a hot cup of coffee over his crotch, he got the idea that she wasn't playing around and bolted out the door."

"Good grief," I groaned, the happy little cloud I'd been floating on all morning suddenly disintegrating. "That's the third one. And it's barely past lunch!"

Megan headed back out to the front and Chloe looked at me with a sympathetic smile. "You know what you're going to have to do, sweetie." I did. But I *really* didn't want to do it, so I groaned again. "Just get it over with, like ripping off a band aid. Quick and painless."

I glared at her. "If you think this is going to be painless, you're sadly mistaken." That earned me another sympathetic look. I ignored it and pulled my cell from my back pocket and dialed a number I so did not want to dial.

"Hey baby girl. To what do I owe the pleasure?" God, my dad sounded so happy, it really was a shame that I was about to burst that bubble.

"Hi, Daddy."

"How's work? The café busy today?"

"Always," I answered with a grin. "But I actually need to ask you a favor. I have a little bit of a problem."

"What problem?" he snapped, automatically going into protective-dad mode.

"Well..." I hesitated, fiddling with a pieces of hair that had fallen from my bun while Chloe mouthed, "*like a band aid*," at me. "You see... there are a bunch of reporters hanging around the restaurant. They're kind of harassing the customers and just being general pains in the ass. I was kind of hoping you could come down here and... I don't know... be all Sherriff and get them to go away?"

"Reporters?" he barked. "The fuck are reporters doing at the café?"

And now came the hard part. Well..."

"Swear to Christ, Eliza, if you don't spit it out, my head's liable to explode. Stop dragging ass and say what you need to say."

So I did. In one really long breath. "Someone took

pictures of me and Ethan at the football game and sold them to the trash magazines saying we were dating, then again at The Moose when he'd had a little too much to drink, saying that we were a couple. We weren't... at least not then, not that I'm a hundred percent sure what we are now, but the magazines didn't seem to care about the truth so they started calling me about doing an interview. Ethan's agent is supposed to be fixing this, but we only found out about the photos yesterday, and now they're all outside the café wanting an exclusive on Ethan Prewitt's new girlfriend, and I'd *really* appreciate if you could just make them go away. You know how much I like my privacy, and they're totally messing with it!"

I sucked in a massive breath once I was finished and waited for my father's reaction... and waited... and waited some more. "Daddy? You there?"

"You telling me my little girl is dating a professional football player?" he asked in a not very nice tone.

"Daddy—"

"A goddamned football player who's known just as well for the number of women he's slept around with as he is for his number of rushing yards?"

"Dad—"

"And I'm just now hearing about it because some

goddamned *reporters* want a story about him dating my *daughter*? Is that what your telling me?"

"Well…"

"Goddamn it, Eliza!" he boomed.

"Don't yell at me!" I boomed back. "I didn't say anything because I'm not really sure *what* we are right now. It's very… new."

"Jesus Christ, baby girl! The man's a total player!"

"He's Ethan, Daddy!" I argued back, the need to defend him outweighing everything else. "He's Ethan, not some football player who screws around. You *know* him. Stop acting like this is some guy you've never met. You've always loved Ethan."

"That was before he put his hands on my fucking daughter," he seethed through the line.

"Dad, just—"

He cut me off. "I'll be there in five minutes."

"What?"

"Five minutes, Eliza. I'll handle the reporters, but then you and I are going to talk."

That sounded like the very last thing I wanted to do, but before I could argue, he'd hung up.

"So…" Chloe came up, throwing her hand over my shoulder. "How'd it go?"

I shot her a killing look before dropping my head

against her shoulder. "It's a toss-up which one of us he's going to kill first."

I felt her shoulders shake with silent laughter. "Oh, sweetie, he's not going to kill either one of you. You know how your dad is. He's just protective. Once he's had a chance to process everything, he'll come around."

"You sound surprisingly optimistic. You didn't hear how he sounded just now. Last time I heard him this pissed, I was thirteen years old and crying because my mother was a raging bitch."

Both her arms came around me in a maternal gesture that I greatly appreciated just then. "You'll talk him around, honey. If this is what you want, he'll eventually see that. He'd never take away any of his girls' happiness. That's not his way."

"But," I started in a small voice, "what if I'm not totally sure this is what I want?"

She pulled back and studied me, a serious expression plastered across her face. "Then we've got bigger problems than your father's head exploding."

My head cocked to the side in confusion. "Why do you say that?"

"Because it would mean those walls you keep up around yourself are more reinforced than I thought." The fact that she sounded so sad when she said that sent a sharp, uncomfortable pang through my chest.

"Chlo—"

"Uh, Eliza?" My head spun around to see Megan peeking through the swinging double door that led into the dining area.

"Yeah?"

"Ethan Prewitt's here. And he looks *pissed*."

My eyes grew wide and I turned to look back at Chloe. She was wearing a similar expression that screamed *oh shit*.

"Batten down the hatches, honey. The shit's about the hit the fan."

Something told me she wasn't wrong about that.

Chapter Twenty-Eight

Ethan

I'D BEEN IN such a good mood. I woke up with the woman I loved in my arms, followed by some world-class sex. Except for the fact that I had to leave her after our shower to make my rehab with Fletch, it had been the best morning of my life.

Then it all went to complete shit when I got a call from my agent while I was on my way to see Eliza. He'd made quick work of getting the name of the person who'd sold those photos to the rags. I wasn't sure why I was so surprised when he told me, I'd known for a long time that Shannon was the lowest form of scum I'd ever met, but realization she'd actually snuck around to take photos of me and Eliza for her own monetary gain had me itching to put my fist through a wall since I couldn't actually put my hands on her.

And things only got worse as I pulled my truck up in front of Sinful Sweets and saw reporters camped out in front of her café. Goddamned vultures. I pushed through the crowd, my jaw ticking and fists clenched in an effort not to go off on the assholes for invading Eliza's privacy. All eyes in the dining room landed on me when I shoved through the glass door.

"Where is she?" I snapped at one of the poor servers.

"Uh... just a second," she mumbled before scurrying off. As I looked out the windows of the restaurant, watching the photographers snapping pictures through the glass, I felt like a caged lion ready to pounce on the next person who was stupid enough to cross my path.

"Ethan?" The sound of Eliza's melodic voice put a stop to my aggravated pacing.

I closed the distance between us and cupped her cheeks in my hands, scanning her face for any signs of distress. "You okay?" I asked in a quiet voice.

Her tiny fingers came up and wrapped around my wrists, and I breathed a sigh of relief when she didn't pull them away. Her face warmed with the most beautiful smile at the same time her fingers tightened. "I'm fine." Her hazel eyes flashed as they skittered throughout the room, landing on the audience of customers who were too interested in what was playing out before them to pretend they weren't eavesdropping. I sensed her discomfort, but didn't give a fuck about nosy people. I needed to make sure she was okay. "What are you doing here? I thought you had therapy."

"Finished early. I got a call from my agent, and I was coming to tell you he found out who sold those pictures when I saw the reporters. Christ, baby. I'm so sorry. Are you all right?"

"Are you serious?" she asked, wide-eyed. "Who?"

My teeth clenched at just the thought of her name. God, I regretted ever getting involved with that bitch. "Shannon."

Eliza's head jerked back. "Are you kidding?!" she squeaked. "Why? How? What a bitch!"

I couldn't help but chuckle at her outrage. It just made her look so damn cute. "I'm going to fix this, baby. I swear."

She still hadn't let go of her anger when she asked, "What the hell did I ever do to her to make her hate me so much?"

My fingers on her face clenched. "Nothing," I answered in a low growl. "Not one damn thing. She's a conniving bitch who's jealous that she'll never be even half as amazing as you are, so she tries to make you feel bad because she can't handle her own pathetic, miserable life."

Eliza's mouth dropped open slightly in surprise at

the fierceness in my tone. My gaze darted to her mouth and there was no stopping myself, I leaned down to press a kiss to those addictive, plump lips just as the piercing sound of a siren broke through my Eliza fog, followed seconds later by a voice that hit me like a cold bucket of ice water.

Eliza's dad.

"I'm going to have to ask all of you to leave the premises!" Derrick called as he stood in the open doorway of the restaurant. "The owner doesn't want any of you loitering around, and seeing as the owner's *my wife*, I'm inclined to give her what she wants. Now get gone before I arrest every one of you for disturbing the peace."

I slung my arm over Eliza's rigid shoulders and watched as one not-so-smart reporter decided it was a good idea to go head to head with Derrick Anderson. I almost felt bad for the guy. "We're perfectly within our rights to be here. We aren't doing anything wrong or disturbing anybody."

Derrick paused before leaning into the café and asking in a loud, booming voice, "Anyone here feeling disturbed?"

Hands went up everywhere. Even Eliza cautiously lifted one up in the air. Derrick turned back to the mouthy paparazzi. "Perks of being in a small town," he said. "I win, you lose. Now get out of here."

They grumbled and bitched, but they all dispersed under the threatening glare of Derrick. Even if the man wasn't the Sherriff, he'd still be intimidating as hell. Within seconds they were gone and the legitimate customers went back to their food and conversation.

But Eliza's body hadn't loosened in my hold, and Derrick looked about two seconds away from committing murder as he stormed over to us. "He knows about us, doesn't he?" I whispered through the side of my mouth.

"Yep," she confirmed, not sounding the least bit happy about whatever was about to go down. Derrick was two feet away when Eliza spoke again. "Daddy—"

"Kitchen. Now," he growled, stomping past us and through a set of swinging double doors.

"Fuck," I muttered at the same time Eliza hissed, "Shit."

Well, no time like the present to face the firing squad.

ELIZA

. . .

For a day that had started out so promising, it really was going to shit much faster than I would have thought possible. As I walked beside Ethan, using the arm he had wrapped around my shoulders as a comforting support, I wracked my brain with ways to try and convince my father to act like a rational adult. Unfortunately, I couldn't come up with a single argument that wouldn't cause his head to explode.

If I had been smarter, I would have disengaged from Ethan's hold since seeing it would only make my father more upset, but as we pushed through the swinging doors into the kitchen, I needed all the strength I could get.

The rest of the kitchen staff, having obviously read the feel of the room correctly seemed to have disbursed for the time being. It wasn't ideal, considering we had a restaurant to run, but I couldn't blame them. That left me, Ethan, Dad, and Chloe alone for the blowup that was about to happen.

I opened my mouth to start, unfortunately Ethan got there before me. "Sir, I just want to say thank you for handling those reporters. If I'd known they were camped out in front of the café, I would have—"

My father cut him off. "You wanna tell me why the hell you're holding on to my daughter like you're more than just friends?"

Oh no. "Dad—"

This time it was Chloe who interrupted. "Good grief, Derrick. Will you take a breath for two seconds and give them a chance to explain?"

My father whirled around. "You knew about this?"

To her credit, Chloe didn't seem the least bit affected by my dad's temper. Ethan, however, had tightened his arm around me like he fully intended on throwing me behind him and out of the line of fire if need be.

"I suspected something's been building between them for a while now, yes. And if you'd have pulled your head out of your ass instead of trying to keep your *grown* daughter a little girl forever, you would have seen it too, and you would have realized it's a good thing!"

"Woman! You knew about this, and didn't say a word about it to me?"

"Man! If you don't want to spend the next several nights getting up close and personal with our sofa, I suggest you put a lid on it!"

I could tell my father wanted to say something else, but having been married to Chloe so long, and obviously being smart, he kept his mouth shut and turned back to me and Ethan.

I started to speak, only to be cut off *again.* "Derrick,"

Ethan started. "I know this wasn't the most ideal way of finding out about our relationship—"

"Son, there's no such thing as an 'ideal way' for me to find out you're dating my daughter. I've always respected the friendship you had with Eliza, but you can't fault me for knowing my daughter deserves better than a man with your kind of reputation with the ladies."

Red flooded my vision at the same time Ethan's body grew completely stiff at my father's insult. "Dad! Stop it!" I stepped away from Ethan's hold and moved closer to my father.

"Baby girl, I'm just looking out for you."

"No, you're not!" I argued. "You're trying to control my life. *That's* what you're doing. I'm not a child anymore, Dad. I'm twenty-two years old. I'm an adult and I get to make my own choices about who I want in my life. You have no say anymore, and that's driving you crazy!"

"Now, that's not fair—"

He started, but I cut him off. "No. What's not fair is you coming in here dead set on ripping into Ethan for daring to touch your precious *baby girl*. What's not fair is you not having faith in me to make smart decisions regarding *my life* and who I allow in it."

"All I know is that my daughter, who'd already experienced enough pain in her life, was annihilated when her best friend up and disappeared for six goddamned years without a word. She walked around like a zombie, pretending that everything was fine, and putting on a mask whenever I was around so she wouldn't worry me with whatever was eating at her."

I sucked in a harsh breath at the pain laced in his words. I had no idea that he'd seen threw the facade I'd put on in front of everyone, and it killed to know I'd hurt him by not talking to him about it. Unfortunately, he wasn't finished, and what he said next flayed me right opened.

"Knowing your child is hurting and won't confide in you is a pain I pray to God you never have to experience, baby girl. But I did. And I might not know the full story, but I know damn good and well that whatever caused that hurt you had behind your eyes had everything to do with him, and I'll be damned if I'm going to let him come back and do it all over again. I could deal with you two picking up your friendship where you left off, but this? This relationship? I just can't stand behind that. I know you're an adult, sweetheart, believe me. But as long as I have breath in my body, I'll do anything and everything in my power to protect you."

I had absolutely no idea what to say. The realization

that I'd been making my father suffer right along with me because I wouldn't tell him what was going on caused my chest to tighten to the point it hurt the breathe.

"Daddy..." my voice trailed off because, for the life of me, I had no clue what to say. Tears fell down my cheeks as something inside of me felt like it as being ripped in two, between Ethan and my father.

"I'm in love with her." At Ethan's sudden exclamation the air in the room grew thicker. We all turned to look at him and what I saw shining in those golden eyes of his, sent an entirely different pain through me. "I'm in love with her, and I know I hurt her, but you have to believe that as long as *I* have breath in *my* body, I'll do whatever it takes to make it up to her so she never has to struggle with that again."

"Those are good words, son. But that's just what they are... words. A real man is judged by his actions, so you'll have to forgive me, but based on your past actions, I'm not carrying much faith in what you're telling me."

"I can respect that, sir," Ethan answered as the muscle in his jaw ticked rapidly. "But you have to know I'm not giving up on Eliza. I'll never give up."

"And you need to know that until I can trust that you're what she needs, I can't stand behind this relationship."

I was suffocating. The air around me was too thick, I couldn't think. The two men who'd mattered most in my life were at a stalemate, over me. I felt like I was being forced to choose between the two of them, and I just couldn't take it. The pressure grew too strong.

"I have to go," I whispered to no one in particular as I kept my head down, moving for the door that would lead me back to the sanctuary of my apartment.

"Eliza..." Ethan grabbed my arm to stop me.

"I can't do this," I whispered, my words breaking as more tears broke free. I looked up at the three people left in the room with me. Ethan looked just as crushed as my father did. Chloe's hands were over her mouth as tears streamed down her face. "This is all too much. First, Shannon messing with my life, and now you and my dad fighting, I just can't. I need to leave. Please let me go."

"Baby, just let me—"

"No!" I interrupted. "I can't choose between you and my father. I can't. This is all too much. I can't handle it. Just let me go."

His face fell, and with it, my own heart dropped to my feet. The instant his fingers loosened I pulled from his grasp and ran, shoving through the door and taking the stairs two at a time.

It wasn't until I was locked inside my apartment and curled up in my bed, with the smell of Ethan on my sheets, that I fully lost it, crying harder than I had in years, pouring all my grief out with every tear that fell onto my pillow.

Chapter Twenty-Nine

Ethan

IT HAD BEEN three days since Eliza ran out of the kitchen of the café in tears. Three fucking days and I felt like I was dying inside. She wasn't answering my calls or texts. With each passing second, I had to tamp down the furious desire to drive over to her place and break the door down and demand she talk to me. But I knew that would only set me back even further than I already was.

I needed to give her space no matter how much it killed me to do so. The foundation we had started to repair was still far from stable, and the shit with Shannon, coupled with her father's disapproval of our relationship, was enough to shake it to its very core. I needed to fix this, but the problem was I had no goddamned clue how to start about doing that.

"Geez, Ethan," my sister's voice called from behind me. "What did that poor, defenseless piece of bread ever do to you?"

At her sarcastic question, I was snatched from my morose thoughts and back into reality. I looked down at the counter where I'd been spreading mayo on a slice of bread for a sandwich and saw that I'd ripped the slice to shreds with my butter knife. With a heavy sigh, I scraped it off the cutting board and threw it in the trash before pulling out another piece and starting over again, hoping Harlow would get bored with my lack of conversation and leave me in peace. I should have known better.

"Want to tell me what's had you walking around in a perpetual state of asshole the past three days?"

"Not in the mood for your attitude, today, Low-Low," I growled as my butter knife tore a hole in the second piece of bread. "Goddamn it!" I shouted, picking it up and flinging it across the room. It splattered against the wall and slowly slid down before finally falling off and hitting the ground with a gross *plop*.

"Okay, that's it," she snapped, coming over and grabbing hold of my elbow, using it to pull me toward the dining room table. "I've let this shit go on for long enough. It's time we talk."

Resting my elbows on the table, I dropped my head

in my hands and began massaging my temples. "No offense Harlow, but this really doesn't have anything to do with you. It's my own shit I'm trying to deal with."

"Bullshit."

My head shot up to see her glaring at me. "I know exactly what this is about. Despite what you think, I'm not stupid, Ethan. I pay attention to what's going on. I know about you and Eliza."

My shoulders slumped in defeat as I sat back in my chair. "You talked to Chloe?"

She nodded. "I did."

"So you know Derrick's less than thrilled about it." It wasn't a question. I could see it in her eyes. She knew, and there was a part of her that probably agreed with him.

"Do you really think this is smart, Ethan? I mean, once your knee's better, you're heading back to Denver. She was in a bad enough state the first time you left."

Christ, I really didn't want to have this conversation with my sister. But with everything that had happened, I didn't see a way out of it. "This time's different," I stated.

"How so? You're still a professional football player with a busy life that lives in a different state. You can't guarantee that the same thing won't happen this time around."

"Yes I can," I argued, that tension that had been

coiling in my gut for days suddenly starting to feel unbearable.

"How?" she demanded loudly. "You left then, and you'll leave again this time. There's no—"

"Because she's not a sixteen year old girl anymore!" I shouted, the words pouring out before I could give them any thought. "I left before because I was falling in love with her. She was just a kid, for Christ's sake. It was fucked up and wrong, and I had no other choice but to disappear before I did something that would ruin both of our futures. But she's not a teenager anymore. She's an adult. *That's* what makes this time different."

"Holy shit," Harlow breathed, her eyes going wide. "That's why you left? Because you were falling for Eliza?"

Resuming my previous position of arms on table, I scrubbed at my face with both hands. "That's part of it."

"Then what was the rest?"

Shit. I really needed to stop speaking before thinking. This was a conversation I never had any intension of having, and I'd just stuck my foot in my mouth. Harlow was like a goddamned dog with a bone. There was no diverting her. "I don't want to talk about this now," I said, standing from the table and moving back to the counter.

"Oh no you don't." She rushed after me and yanked

the loaf of bread from my hand, tossing it back into the breadbasket. "I don't feel like going to the store today because you want to take your frustrations out on food products. Besides, you can't just drop a bombshell like that and think I'm going to let it slide. You brought it up. Now spill."

Like a said, a dog with a bone. "Harlow, just let it go."

"Screw that! You've been dodging this conversation for six freaking years, Ethan! What other reasons did you have for not coming home?"

"The reasons are my own!" I insisted. "Just leave it."

Getting in my face, my sister gave my chest a shove. "Tell me, damn it!"

And with that, I snapped. "Because of you!"

Her expression morphed into one of immense pain, and I hated myself for hurting her. "Because of me?" she asked in a small, heartbroken voice.

"Fuck! Harlow, I never wanted to have this goddamned conversation because I never wanted to see this look on your face."

Her golden-brown eyes swam with tears as she sniffled. "Well excuse me for being upset when I just found out my baby brother abandoned home because he didn't want to be around me. You'll have to forgive me for having my heart broken!" she snapped back, turning on her heels in an attempt to storm out of the kitchen.

I couldn't possibly let her leave thinking that I had wanted nothing to do with her. Grabbing her by the arm, I spun her back around and pinned her to my chest, holding tight as she started to struggle. "That's not it," I whispered into the hair at the top of her head. "That's not it at all, Low-Low. I love you more than anything. It wasn't that I didn't want to be around you. I swear."

She pulled back enough to look up at me, sniffling and batting at the few tears that had broken free. "Then what was it *exactly?* And you better make it good, or so help my God, Ethan, I'm going to punch you right in the throat."

I couldn't help but smile at my sister's tough girl act. "You have to actually listen, okay? Don't interrupt. Just let me say what I have to say before you lay into me." She huffed but nodded her head. That wasn't good enough. I knew her too well. "Promise."

She rolled her eyes dramatically, but said, "Fine. I promise."

Leading her back to the table, I pulled out a chair for her and took the one right next to her. My only option was to just dive right in, so that's what I did. "I left because I thought I needed to build a life for myself where I'd never be stuck depending on someone else. I thought that was the only way I could guarantee I'd have the security I never had growing up." She opened her mouth to speak, but I held up my hand to stop her. "I'm not saying it was a rational way of thinking, but it was *mine*. Our parents died and we were forced to leave everything we knew to come here and live with Gram. It was good for a while, but then, one day, you just... left. I get why *now*. I understand that you needed an escape, but back then, I was just a kid. I felt like you abandoned me, and that killed, Low-Low.

"I eventually let that go, but when Gram died that just brought all those feelings back to the surface." I leaned over and grabbed her hands in mine, holding tight. "You came back, and not a day goes by that I don't love you for giving up your whole life to come and take care of me. But once you got here, you and Noah started up again almost instantly. Then if felt like I blinked and you were pregnant with Lucy. Noah moved in, and you guys had your very own family to worry about. The two of you never once made me feel like I was unwanted, but, subconsciously, I felt like I didn't belong. This went from being my home with Gram to being yours and Noah's. I felt like I was just a guest in your lives. I left because I wanted something that was just *mine*. Something I knew I wouldn't lose. But I never, *ever* stopped loving you. I never resented you or Noah. I was so glad you'd finally found your own happiness. But at the same time, I was struggling to find my own. Once my feelings for Eliza started to change, I couldn't handle everything I was feeling. It was the coward's way out, but I decided to just run and leave it all behind."

I gave her hands another squeeze, imploring her with my eyes to understand. "I'm so damn sorry if what I did hurt you."

She remained silent for several seconds, clearly fighting—and losing—against crying. Finally, in a move that was so fast it startled me, she jerked her hands from mine and shot from her chair. "You jerk!" she shouted, planting both her palms on my shoulders and pushing. "You stupid jerk! Why didn't you ever say anything? I could have fixed it if you'd have just told me, you... you... stupid—"

"Jerk. I get it," I said, standing to my full height and grabbing her hands to stop the blows she was landing. "I'm a stupid jerk. I know."

Some of the fire drained from her and she quit hitting me, moving in and wrapping her arms around my waist in a tight hug. "Gah! If you would have just said something..."

"Like what?" I asked on a small laugh, hugging her back. "That I was unhappy because my sister had finally found happiness? I might be an asshole, but I'm not *that* big an asshole."

"Shut up," she mumbled against my chest, pulling one hand back to give me another weak smack. "You're not an asshole."

"You really think so?"

She breathed in deep, still holding on tight. "I know so. But I hate that you spent so long struggling with that, shrimp."

The use of her old nickname for me warmed me from the inside out, causing my arms holding her to squeeze. "I'm sorry I never said anything," I whispered against her head.

"I'm sorry too." She leaned back, not breaking our hold, and looked up into my eyes. "You know I love you, right? So damn much. I know you're my brother, but I always felt like you were *mine*, just like Lucy and Evan. I hate the fact I made you feel any differently."

"You didn't," I said fiercely. "It was never anything you did, Harlow. It was shit in my own head that I needed to get worked out. You and Noah both were never anything but good to me, and despite everything I just told you, I grew up feeling loved. You have to know that."

She searched my face for several seconds before

finally accepting the sincerity shining in my eyes. "Okay," she whispered.

"And I love you, too. Even though you can be a *total* pain in my ass most of the time."

At that, she laughed and disengaged from my hold. I watched as she moved to the counter, grabbed the loaf of bread, and began making a sandwich. Once she was done, she carried the plate over to me and held it out. "Here. Eat. And let's figure out a way for you to finally get *your* happiness."

Christ, but I loved my sister something crazy.

Chapter Thirty

Eliza

"You okay?" Chloe asked, coming up to me in the kitchen and slinging her arm across my shoulders.

I wasn't, not really. But over the past three days, I'd had the chance to do a lot of thinking, and in spite of everything that had gone down days before with Ethan, myself, and my father, there was one thing about that entire conversation I couldn't stop thinking about.

There weren't many men who would have had the courage to stand up in front of my father, but Ethan had. And even with all the horrible things my father said, he'd *still* had the guts to tell him he was in love with me, and that he'd do everything in his power to prove himself. To me, that in itself spoke volumes about the *actions* my father was so intent on shoving down Ethan's throat. He stood toe to toe with my father and never backed down.

It had taken me longer than it should have, but I felt like I'd finally managed to pull my head out of *my* ass and see what was right in front of me.

"There's something I want to talk to you about," I said, turning away from the stove to face Chloe, full on.

"Yeah? And what's that, sweetheart?"

"What do you think..." God, I really wasn't sure what to say. It was such a huge request, such a massive gesture. But the one thing I'd discovered over the past three days was that Ethan Prewitt was worth a massive gesture. "How would you feel about... expanding?"

Her brows dipped down in confusion, "Expanding what?"

"The café," I answered quietly. "I know what I'm about to request is a big deal, and it'll take some time for you to consider, but what do you think about opening another café in, say, Denver?"

Anxiety clawed at my insides as her expression morphed from bewilderment, to excitement, before finally settling on what could only be described as complete exuberance. "I think... that's a *fantastic* idea!" she shouted excitedly. "That is, if you're considering expanding to a café in Denver for the reason I *think* you are."

"Well," I giggled, her excitement for me growing contagious. "If you think it's because I finally realized I'm in love with Ethan and want to be with him, then you'd be right."

Chloe threw her hands in the air and began squealing so loud I cringed before pulling me into a hug and bouncing from foot to foot. "Oh my God! This is so amazing!"

"Thanks," I laughed, pulling away once she'd managed to compose herself. "I think so, too." Some of my exuberance dwindled at my next thought. "Now I just have to find a way to convince Dad this is a good thing."

"Oh, sweetie, don't you worry about your father," she said, cupping my cheeks. "When he sees that Ethan makes you happy, really and truly happy, he'll come around. I promise. That's all he's ever wanted for you."

I bit at my bottom lip, considering what she was saying. "You think?"

"Honey, I know." She smiled. "Trust me, I've been with your father long enough to learn a thing or two. Behind that gruff exterior your dad's a teddy bear. You know that."

I giggled again, because I really, *really* did.

"Eliza?" Chloe and I were pulled from the moment at the sound of Megan's voice. We turned to look at her and both of us grew still at the concern marring her face. "There's someone out here asking for you."

Chloe rolled her eyes and grabbed my hand. "Let's go get whatever latest drama is waiting out of the way, then we can talk details of opening Sinful Sweets Café, Denver addition."

I laughed and followed her out, my heart full to bursting all because of the amazing woman who played such an intricate part in raising me. However, that euphoric feeling was smashed to smithereens at the sight of the person waiting for us on the other side of the door.

"You've got to be kidding me," I grumbled under my breath at the sight of Shannon, standing there with an evil cat-that-caught-the-canary grin on her bitter face. "I'm pretty sure I've made myself pretty clear on how I feel about you in my establishment. Please tell me you have a really good reason for souring my day with your presence."

I hadn't thought it was possible, but that that demented smile on her face actually managed to grow. "Oh, I've got *the best* reason. See, I was just shopping at Mabel's, minding my one business when someone came in asking where she could find you." My gut was telling me that the glee on her face didn't bode well for me, but she wasn't finished. "Now, seeing as everyone in this town knows the story, I know that it's been *years* since you've seen her, so I felt it only right to bring her here so you could have your happy little family reunion."

At her words, ice filled my veins and I froze in place as a woman I hadn't seen since I was a girl stood from one of the tables and came up next to Shannon. I vaguely heard Chloe suck in a huge gasp over the blood rushing through my ears.

My voice came out strangled as I addressed the one person I never thought I'd lay eyes on again. "Mom?"

"Hello, darling."

ETHAN

I DIDN'T HAVE A SCRIPT PREPARED FOR WHAT I HAD to say, but I was still riding the high from my conversation with Harlow, feeling relief that that two-ton weight I'd been carrying on my shoulders for years was finally gone. I knew it would take time and work for me and my family to fully come to get to the place I wanted us to be, but we made our start earlier today. So on the wave of that, I was ready to take care of the last thing keeping me from grabbing hold of my happiness and never letting go.

"Can I help you?" the woman at the front desk asked politely once I'd pushed through the glass doors.

"Uh, yeah. I was actually wondering if Sherriff Anderson was in. I'd like to speak with him."

"Oh, yes, sure. He's back in his office. Let me just ring him for you." I tried not to shift from foot to foot as she picked up the phone and hit a few buttons that would connect her with Derrick. "Yes, hi, Sherriff, there's a..."

"Ethan Prewitt," I filled in for her when she glanced up at me.

"Yes, there's an Ethan Prewitt to see you? Yes. Yes. Okay." She hung up the phone and looked at me with a bright smile. "He'll be right up."

A few seconds later the sound of boots hitting the tile floor sounded through the front lobby. Shoving my hands in my pockets to keep from fidgeting as Derrick Anderson rounded the corner, coming to a stop, his hands resting on his waist, dangerously close to the gun on his belt.

"Well, have to say, this is a surprise." And not a happy one, judging by his tone. "What can I do for you, Ethan?"

"I was wondering if we could talk..." My eyes scanned back to the woman who was sitting at the front desk, watching us with rapt fascination. "In private?"

Derrick's hands came off his hips as he crossed his arms over his chest. "I've got a busy schedule, son, so if you'd just say what you need—"

"Oh, no you don't Sherriff," the woman chirped happily. "Your whole afternoon's free and clear."

"Thanks a lot, Marlene," he ground out to the oblivious receptionist before turning on his heels with a sigh. "All right, let's go get this over with."

I followed him down the long hall and through the bullpen area before coming to stop at his office door. He stood to the side and waved his hand for me to enter, then came in behind me and closed the door before moving around his desk and taking a seat. I sat in one of the small, uncomfortable chairs on the other side and braced for whatever was about to happen.

"Just so you know, if you're here to discuss your relationship with Eliza, I stand by what I said the other day. I don't support the two of you being together."

Squaring my shoulders and lifting my chin, I sucked in a breath and said what I'd come to say, whether he wanted to hear it or not. "I respect your opinion, Derrick, but I'm not here to ask your permission."

At that, his entire frame got tight. "Excuse me?"

"I'm not here for your permission to see your daughter. I respect you more than you could ever know, and for Eliza's sake, I hope that one day you can accept our relationship, but sir, I'm in love with your daughter, and there isn't a damn thing I won't do to keep her. I know I hurt her six years ago, and if she'll let me, I'll spend the rest of my life trying to make up for it, but I'm not giving her up. She makes me happy, but more, I know, if given the chance *I* can make *her* happy. And that's what I intend to do."

Sitting back in his chair, he steepled his fingers and studied me with an intensity the likes of which I'd never experienced before. "Thinking you should probably tell me what it was that caused you to break my little girl in the first place, son."

I'd been expecting that question from him, but that didn't mean I was any more excited about giving him the answer, especially considering he was wearing a *fucking gun*. But if I had any chance of winning the man who meant the world to Eliza over, I was going to have to give him everything.

"You know I cared for your daughter growing up. She was my best friend. I treated her like I would my own sister." *Shit, now comes the hard part. Please don't let him fucking shoot me.* "Before I entered the draft, my feelings for Eliza started to change. I knew it wasn't right," I hurried to add when I saw his face begin to grow red. "I knew she was too young, and I never would have dreamed about doing anything about it, but that's the truth. I was starting to fall for your daughter, sir, and it scared the hell out of me."

"Jesus fucking Christ," he sighed, sitting back in his chair and rubbing at his forehead with one hand.

"I don't know if there was a better way for me to have handled it, but I did the only thing I could think of at the time, which was to remove myself from the situation. I hate that I hurt her in the process, you've got to believe that. But what I need you to understand is that I've loved Eliza for a very long time, and I'd give up *everything* for her. There isn't anything I wouldn't do for her. That includes admitting my feelings for her to her Sherriff father, all the while knowing he'd be within his rights to put a bullet in my ass."

Derrick remained silent for several seconds as he let everything I'd just laid on him absorb. "Fuck me," he finally mumbled. "And she knows about this?"

"She knows everything," I admitted. "I'll never keep another secret from her again. I swear that."

I was prepared to make more promises, including, but not limited to, naming our first born child after him, when my cellphone chimed from my pocket. Thinking it could be Eliza responding to one of the millions of messages I left her, I yanked it out and engaged the screen, only to have my blood run cold at what I read.

Standing to my feet so fast the chair I'd been sitting

in flew backward, I shoved my phone back in my jeans and looked at Derrick. "Let's go."

"What? Where?" He asked, coming out of his own chair.

"The café. That was Chloe. Shannon showed up to ambush Eliza."

Derrick growled as he rounded the desk. "That fucking girl. Never did understand what you saw in her."

"I was a young, dumb kid. Not that that's an excuse." I came to a stop at the mouth of the hallway, putting my hand on his shoulder to stop him. "But there's something else I need to tell you, and you need to keep your head. Got me?"

"Just spit it out, Ethan."

Then I said the one thing that was bad enough to make me and the Sherriff of Pembrooke lose our collective shit.

"Shannon's there with Eliza's mother."

Chapter Thirty-One

Eliza

I COULDN'T MOVE. I couldn't think. I couldn't form a fucking sentence. And all the while I felt like I was trapped in my own personal Hell, Shannon was positively delirious with excitement that she'd just managed to fuck everything up for me... *once again.*

"Eliza. Eliza, honey. Talk to me," Chloe coaxed from my side. Her sweet, worried voice was enough to pull me from my melancholy.

"Oh my God," I turned to her and choked. "I can't handle this. I can't handle it."

She put an arm around my waist and held me to her side. "It's okay, sweetie. It's okay."

I didn't know how she could say that. Standing in front of my mother, I was *anything* but okay. And she couldn't have been much better, seeing as it was the same woman who'd trashed her bakery and hit her with a car years ago.

"Eliza, darling," my mother started, but I clamped my hands over my ears, squeezed my eyes closed, and shook my head, unaware I looked like I was having a mental breakdown in front of God and everybody.

"No," was all I managed to get out when the door to the café swung opened so fast the glass almost broke. Before I could process what was happening, Ethan came barreling in with my father close on his heels.

"Upstairs," he growled menacingly as he pulled me from Chloe's hold and held me to him. "We're not doing this shit down here with a goddamned audience." Then, without further ado, he picked me up, in front of *God and everybody*, and carried me through the kitchen and out the door that led to the internal stairwell.

"Ethan," I whispered, still feeling somewhat hysterical.

"Not yet, baby," he returned as he took the stairs at a surprisingly fast clip. Once we reached the top, he put me to my feet. "Keys, sweetheart."

By the look on his face, I knew it wouldn't be smart to argue, so I pulled the key from my back pocket and deposited it in his waiting hand. In a blink, he had the door unlocked and thrown open, ushering me inside.

Seconds later, the door slammed closed and I looked around the room to see it was filled with me, Ethan, my father and Chloe, my *mother*, and that bitch from Hell, Shannon.

"Right," Ethan spit before anyone else could say a word. "First things first." He left my side just long enough to get in Shannon's face. "Just when I thought you couldn't possibly get any fucking lower, you go and pull a stunt like this."

To her credit, she at least had the decency to pale under Ethan's terrifying demeanor. "Ethan—"

"Shut the fuck up!" he bellowed. "You don't get to talk. I'm going to tell you how it's going to be from here on out, then you're going to get the fuck away from Eliza, and so help me God, she better never lay eyes on you again. I know it was you who sold those photos to the tabloids. I know it was the bullshit *you* fed them that was posted online. And I swear to fucking Christ, Shannon, if I ever find out you've taken another picture of us without our permission, I'll slap you with a goddamn harassment and stalking charge!" She swallowed so thickly I could see her throat moving, but Ethan wasn't done yet. "There is no amount of money I won't spend, no resources I won't utilize to bury you if I so much as hear you *looked* at Eliza in a way she doesn't like. And sweetheart, I'm fucking rich, so you better believe I'll spend every goddamned dime I have to ruin *your fucking life*. Do I make myself clear?"

"Eth—"

"Yes or no question. Do I make myself clear!?" he finished on a roar.

"Y-yes," she stuttered, looking about two seconds away from bursting into tears.

"Good. Now get the fuck out," he hissed. She didn't hesitate, turning and running for the door, and something told me Shannon wasn't a person I'd ever have to worry about again.

"Ethan," I whispered, breaking him from his rage and drawing his attention back to me. He moved so fast I didn't have a chance to take a step back before he was on me, his arms wrapping around my waist and pinning me to his side as he turned us to face the one other person in my apartment that I didn't want there.

"Now you," he said, sounding no less angry, even with the absence of Shannon The Bitch. "What the fuck are you doing here?"

My mother, never one to be cowed by someone she felt was inferior to her, squared her shoulders and lifted her chin in an effort to look down her nose at Ethan. No small feat seeing as he towered over her. I noticed then that in all the years that had passed, she was still no less beautiful. But her eyes remained hard and uncaring, just as they'd been when I was a child. Whatever brought her back to Pembrooke had nothing to do with a loving Mother-Daughter reunion.

"I'm here to speak with my daughter, if you don't mind," she said in an ice-cold voice.

"Well I fucking mind, Layla," my father chimed in. "You haven't had fuck all to say to her in nine years and you think you can just waltz your ass back into town and demand a face to face?"

"I don't see how it's any of your business, Derrick," she hissed. Hate radiated from her entire frame as she looked back and forth between my father and Chloe. "She's *my* daughter, too."

"No she's not," Chloe replied, sounding madder than I'd ever heard before. "She's *my* daughter. *Not yours. I* was the one who held her when she cried. *I* was the one that taught her to cook. *I* was the one who helped pick her up when you almost ruined her! *I* was the one who loved her unconditionally. She's *my daughter!*"

My breath hitched at everything she'd just said, and I couldn't help but cry as I watched tears course down her cheeks as my father moved to hold her the same way Ethan was holding me. God, *God.* She was right. Chloe was my mother in every single way that counted. I'd always loved her, always would, but it wasn't until that very moment that I realized just how deep that love ran.

"Baby," Ethan called, breaking into my thoughts. "Is there anything this woman has to say that you want to hear?"

"No," I whispered with a shake of my head. Because there wasn't. There wasn't a single solitary word I wanted to hear from her. The thirteen-year-old girl who'd once wanted nothing more than for her mother to love her had grown up. And I had so much love in my life already that I didn't need anything from her anymore.

"Eliza—" my mother started.

"You heard her," Ethan cut her off. "She doesn't want to hear whatever shit you have to say."

For the first time ever, I saw my mother express something other than superiority and hate. Cold, hard fear. "Eliza, please," she said, pushing past everyone to get to me. "My last husband divorced me. I have nothing left. *Nothing*. He left me penniless! I saw those pictures of you and your Ethan, and I knew you were doing well. I knew you'd made a life for yourself and were happy. I just thought—"

"You thought you'd try and dig your way back into your daughter's life in an effort to get to her man's money," Ethan voiced the words I was just thinking, sounding just as disgusted as I felt. "Christ, I take it back. I thought no one could get lower than Shannon, but I see I was wrong. There's a special place in Hell for bitches like you."

At that, Chloe choked on a laugh, having to slap her hands over her mouth in an attempt to keep it in. And that warmth that had started blooming in my chest at her heartfelt declaration suddenly exploded, shrouding me like a comforting, loving blanket. With Ethan, my father, Chloe, and the rest of my loved ones, I realized I had it all. I didn't need anyone else. There was room in my heart, sure, and as long as I had them with me, I knew I was safe to let others in because they'd always be there to protect me. But I didn't *need* anyone else, because standing in the apartment of my living room, in that very moment, I realized I had *everything*.

I was happy.

"Fuck me," my father seethed. "How I managed to make such perfection with the likes of you is beyond me, but I thank Christ every single day that your poison never infested my girl. She's everything you're not."

God, and the feels just kept on coming!

"You need money?" Ethan cut in. "I'll give you money. I'll write you a nice fat check to get the fuck out of our lives and never darken Eliza's doorway again. Her peace of mind that she'll never have to see your face is worth more than anything to me." It was when he began to pull away from me and reached for his back pocket that I finally came out of my daze and jumped into action.

"No." At the sound of my voice, everyone paused and turned to me. My mother, who looked ecstatic just one second ago started to look worried again.

Ethan leaned in close, "What, baby?"

"No. Don't write her a check." I disengaged from Ethan's arms and moved to stand before my mother. "He's not giving you anything. You don't deserve a single cent from him, but he'd have given it to you... *for me*," I whispered, leaning in closer. "Because he's a good person, the very best kind, and he loves me, he'd have done it. But I won't let him, because I've just realized something myself. He loves me because *I'm* a good person and I deserve it. He loves me because I'm worth loving. You've done nothing in your entire life to earn that kind of devotion from anyone. So I'll be *damned* if I let the man *I love* give you *anything*. I'm done with you. I never want to see you again. And when you're laying in your bed at night, bitter and alone, I hope you know that I'll be surrounded by people I love, who love me back, because I was worth it."

With that, I'd said everything I ever needed to say to the woman who gave birth to me. I moved back to Ethan, but not before looking in my father's direction, pride shining deep in his eyes. "Please get her out of my house. She isn't welcome here."

"Gladly, baby girl."

I walked straight into Ethan's arms and wrapped my own around his waist, holding on for dear life. "I love you," I whispered against the heat of his chest.

"I love you too, Eliza," he said against the crown of my head. "Always will."

Pulling back slightly, I looked up at him, the vision of him blurry through my unshed tears. "I'm sorry it took me so long to pull my head out of my ass," I whispered, earning a deep, vibrating chuckle from him.

"Better late than never, sweetheart. I'm just glad to be hearing it now."

The apartment door opened and closed. "Well," my dad spoke up, interrupting our moment. "That's done, so I better be getting back down to the station. Need to make sure that woman actually leaves town." My father made his way toward us and leaned in to press a kiss to my cheek. "Love you, baby girl. And so damn proud of you."

"I love you too, Dad," I told him with a watery smile.

"Son," he said, facing Ethan and holding his hand out. "We'll see you at dinner Sunday."

"Yes sir," Ethan responded, shaking my father's hand.

"Wait, Sunday?" I cut in.

My father's expression melted into one of approval as Chloe came up and wrapped her arms around him. "Family dinner. Can't have one of those without your man there, now can we?"

Just like that, Ethan had earned my father's acceptance, giving me the very last piece I needed to finish building my own happiness.

Chapter Thirty-Two

Ethan

"Honey, what are you doing?" Eliza giggled from behind me as I dragged her through the woods. Christ, I'd never get used to that beautiful sound. She'd been mine, completely mine for the past few weeks, and every moment I woke up with her in my arms, I had to pull her closer to convince myself it wasn't all a dream.

I'd been waiting for the perfect moment to ask her to be mine for the rest of our lives, and this was it. After spending a blissful, yet somewhat chaotic Thanksgiving with both of our families at her father's house—my sister having been banned from the kitchen, thank God—I'd finally found the opportunity to pull Derrick aside and ask his permission to marry his baby girl. He made me sweat for a few minutes before finally slapping me on the back and welcoming me to the family, and that led to the here and now.

I pulled her to a stop once we reached our destination. The sun was just beginning to set over the lake, painting the sky in the most amazing colors. I couldn't have possibly timed it better.

"God," Eliza breathed, releasing my hand to walk closer to the edge. "I haven't been up here in years. I'd forgotten how beautiful this place is."

"Me too," I mumbled, coming up behind her, breathing in that glorious scent of almonds and vanilla. "You know, I always thought of this as our spot."

"I did too," she whispered. I wrapped one arm around her waist and, with my other hand, pulled out the ring that had been burning a hole in my pocket all evening.

"That's why I couldn't have imagined doing this anywhere else." I held the ring out in front of her. Her body went tight for a second before she spun around in my arms, her hazel eyes dancing with the happiness I'd put there. I couldn't imagine a better feeling in the world.

"Are you serious?"

I chuckled and lifted her left hand to slide the ring into place. "Never been more serious about anything in my entire life. Eliza Anderson, I've loved you for as long as I can remember, and I can't imagine there ever coming a day when I won't love you even more than the last. Will you give me my happiness and be my wife?"

"Yes!" she shouted, throwing herself in my arms as she peppered kisses all across my face. "Oh my God!" She threw her head back and yelled, "I'm getting married!"

I held her to me for several seconds, enjoying the feel of her against me before finally forcing myself to pull back. "That's not all, baby."

"What could you possibly have left?" she laughed.

"This," I answered holding my arms out at my sides.

Her eyebrows dipped and her head tipped to the side in confusion. "Huh?"

"This. All of this," I stated looking around *our spot*. "I bought this land not too long ago and have been in contact with a few contractors. Baby, at this very moment, you're standing in our living room."

She clamped her hands over her mouth and spun around in a circle. "You didn't."

"I did." I nodded, making my way back to her so I could hold her against me. "Construction starts at the beginning of the year. Welcome home, sweetheart."

"Oh my God," she whispered, tears swimming in her eyes. "That's just... I can't..." Placing her hands on my chest, she suddenly looking worried. "But Ethan, what about your career?"

"Fuck football." I locked my wrists together at her back so she couldn't pull away. "Football means nothing to me if I don't have you in my life, Eliza. I said I'd bend over backward and do whatever I had to show you I loved you, and that's what I'm doing. Your life is here. *You're* here. So this is where I want to be."

"But—"

"No buts. I've thought long and hard about this, baby. This is what I want."

"I get that," she started. "And I love you so much for wanting to give this to me. But what about the café?"

My head jerked back and it was my turn to be confused. "What about it?"

"Well, it's just that if we're *here* who's going to run the café Chloe and I are opening in Denver?"

"What?" I froze solid as a sneaky smile stretched across her beautiful face.

"Surprise," she giggled. "You see I'm in love with a man who's kind of a big deal football player back in Denver. It's always been his dream, and since I'm such a wonderful fiancée, I never would have considered asking him to give that up. I *too* have been in talks with a few contractors, along with Chloe, and *we're* breaking ground on Sinful Sweets Café, Denver at the beginning of the year.

I was having trouble processing everything I'd just heard. "Are you... you can't be serious."

"Oh, I'm dead serious," she said. "And since there seems to have been a lack of communication on each of our part, I figure there's only on solution for our little problem."

I couldn't help but smile as I leaned down and kissed her lips. "And that would be?"

"During the season, we live in Denver. During off-season, *this* is our home," she replied, hold her arms out wide. "See? Perfect solution."

I chuckled against her mouth. "Thank God I'm marrying someone so smart."

She nodded. "Exactly. Now, Ethan Prewitt, football star. Do me a favor."

"Anything, baby."

"I was hoping you'd say that." She gave me a quick kiss and took one step back. "Make love to me in our living room."

That, I could definitely do.

Epilogue

Eliza

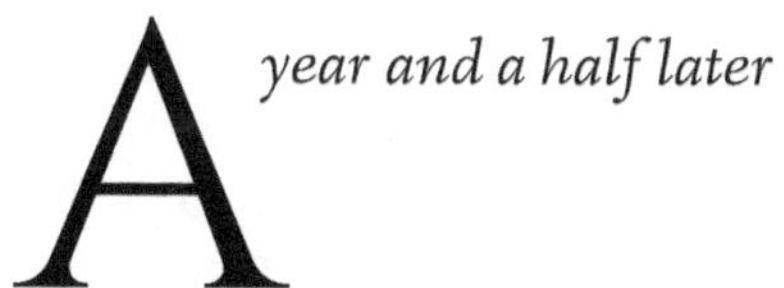

A *year and a half later*

"Move your ass, baby! If we don't get on the road now, we're going to be late!"

"I'm coming!" I yelled back, throwing the last of my clothes into my suitcase and rushing around the bed to snatch the picture of the two of us Ethan had kept on his bedside table all these years. I tossed it on top of everything and zipped the bag closed.

"Geez, woman. Your father's already been staring daggers at me since I knocked you up. If we're late to family dinner, he's going to shoot my ass on sight." I laughed as I gave the suitcase a yank, only to groan when the weight refused to budge off the bed. "Here, let me get it." Pressing a kiss to my lips as he walked by—just as he always did whenever I was near—Ethan pulled the suitcase off the bed and dropped it to the floor.

"Good Christ. What the hell did you pack?"

"Hey! Don't give me shit. This is off-season. We'll be in Pembrooke for months, I need my things."

"I can buy you more things, there. There's no need to pack up the entire condo, baby."

"I didn't pack up the whole condo," I glared. "That's just the important stuff."

He laughed and began wheeling the bag out of the room, kissing me on the way. "Whatever you say. Now can we please go so your dad doesn't send out a search party?"

"You're over exaggerating," I told him with a roll of my eyes. "He hasn't hated you since before we got married."

Ethan let out a disgruntled grunt. "Then you clearly didn't see his face when we told him he was going to be a grandfather. I thought the man was going to have a coronary at the thought of me defiling his precious daughter."

I couldn't help but laugh because he wasn't exaggerating. You'd have thought my father believed we'd been living as a married couple for the past year complete with separate bedrooms. "Yeah, well, I think he's lightened up since your team won the Super Bowl. The bragging rights with that alone are enough to buy you at least a year of no death threats."

We locked the door to the condo and headed toward the elevator. "You'd think," Ethan grumbled, pressing the down button and slinging his arm over my shoulder as we waited. "But just to be on the safe side, all the paperwork for our life insurance policies are in the lockbox on the top closet shelf. Use the money wisely."

He winked and I smacked him in his nice, firm stomach as the doors opened and we climbed onto the elevator. With my head resting against his shoulder, I thought back over the past year and a half.

Shortly after proposing, Ethan had insisted we get married right away. We argued about it... *a lot*, but ended up getting married on our spot just before Christmas—despite the chilling temperature—with the reception being held at my dad and Chloe's house. It was the most perfect wedding. Small, intimate, and quick, just us surrounded by the people who loved us the most. Since he was still out for the season, we spent the holidays and the following summer bouncing between Pembrooke and Denver so I could check on the progress of the new café and begin the hiring process.

I'd lucked out in finding a general manager who could run the place in her sleep, so moving back home during the off-season wasn't such a terrifying idea now that I knew the restaurant wouldn't burn to the ground in my absence.

I could honestly say that I'd never been happier in my life than I have been married to Ethan Prewitt, football star, and every morning I wake up thankful that we both managed to find our way back to each other.

I loved him as a child, and that love eventually turned into the most important friendship I'd ever had. We lost our footing for a few years, but we found our way home, and I was happy to say our relationship had come full circle.

The elevator dinged and my husband took my hand, leading me through the parking garage toward our car. "Did you call Lilly to tell her we were coming?" he asked as he popped the truck and put the last of our bags in.

"Yep. And she can't wait. She said she's been dying to rub my belly ever since she visited last month."

We climbed in, buckled up, and Ethan started the car. "You ever find out what went down with her and Quinn?"

I frowned at the reminder. Lilly called me around last Christmas in tears over a guy she'd been dating. She didn't go into detail, but she eventually let it slip that she'd been seeing Quinn for a few months and it had ended badly. "No," I answered. "Did you ever ask him about it?"

"I did, but he was suspiciously tight lipped about the whole thing."

I gave that some thought. "I don't like this. Quinn's a good guy. I can't imagine what he could have done to make her so upset."

Knowing how much it bothered me that my best friend was in pain, Ethan reached over and took my hand in his, lifted it to his lips and placed a kiss on my knuckles, right where his ring rested. "Well, no worries baby. We're heading home now, so you have all the time in the world to meddle in her business."

I laughed at that. "It's only fair. She did the same with us."

"That she did," Ethan grinned, giving my hand a squeeze before resting it on his thigh. "And I couldn't be happier about the outcome."

"Me either," I smiled as we turned out of the garage and onto the road that would lead us home.

"I love you, Ethan Prewitt."

He gave me a quick look, gracing me with that smile that got me every single time. "And I love you, Eliza Prewitt. Always have and always will."

I let that rest in my soul and warm me from the inside out because I had no doubt that he meant it.

I took his hand and rested both our palms on my protruding belly. Together, we'd found our happiness. And it was the most beautiful thing imaginable.

The End

More Pembrooke Titles

When Derrick Anderson moved from Jackson Hole to the small town of Pembrooke, he did it determined to wipe the slate clean. After eight years spent trapped in a miserable marriage, he's made a vow to never take the plunge again. He wants to be untethered, not tangled up in the strings that come with a committed relationship. He has his daughter, his career, and an ex-wife hell bent on making his life unbearable. His plate is already full. The only problem is, he didn't have a plan in place to protect his heart from her.

Neither of them were prepared for the course their lives would take. But once a rollercoaster begins to move, you can't just climb off, now can you?

The only thing they can do is strap in, hold on tight, and enjoy the ride.

A Broken Soul

He's terrified of loving her.

Quinn Mallick already had his happily-ever-after, and in the blink of an eye it was ripped away from him. Now he's content to walk through the rest of his life carrying the weight of that guilt on his shoulders. He's convinced he doesn't deserve a second chance. But when the town's beautiful dance teacher turns her sights on him he finds himself questioning everything.

She's terrified of losing him.

Lilly Mathewson's once quiet, predictable life has been turned on its head. Feeling alone and adrift, she finds her comfort in the most unexpected of places. Falling for the town widower was never part of the plan, but there is just something about the temperamental man she can't seem to let go of.

What started as two grieving people leaning on each other has quickly turned into something neither of them expected. Lilly is ready to take the next step, but how do you move forward when the man you love refuses to let go of the past?

Especially when the only hope they have of healing their broken souls is if they do it together.

Discover Other Books by Jessica

<u>WHITECAP SERIES</u>
Crossing the Line
My Perfect Enemy

<u>WHISKEY DOLLS SERIES</u>
Bombshell
Knockout
Stunner
Seductress
Temptress
Vamp

<u>HOPE VALLEY SERIES:</u>
Out of My League
Come Back Home Again

The Best of Me
Wrong Side of the Tracks
Stay With Me
Out of the Darkness
The Second Time Around
Waiting for Forever
Love to Hate You
Playing for Keeps
When You Least Expect It
Never for Him

REDEMPTION SERIES

Bad Alibi
Crazy Beautiful
Bittersweet
Guilty Pleasure
Wallflower
Blurred Line
Slow Burn
Favorite Mistake
Sweet Spot

THE CLOVERLEAF SERIES:

Picking up the Pieces
Rising from the Ashes
Pushing the Boundaries

Worth the Wait

THE COLORS NOVELS:
Scattered Colors
Shrinking Violet
Love Hate Relationship
Wildflower

THE LOCKLAINE BOYS (a LOVE HATE RELATIONSHIP spinoff):
Fire & Ice
Opposites Attract
Almost Perfect

THE PEMBROOKE SERIES (a WILDFLOWER spinoff):
Sweet Sunshine
Coming Full Circle
A Broken Soul

CIVIL CORRUPTION SERIES
Corrupt
Defile
Consume
Ravage

<u>GIRL TALK SERIES:</u>

Seducing Lola

Tempting Sophia

Enticing Daphne

Charming Fiona

<u>STANDALONE TITLES:</u>

One Knight Stand

Chance Encounters

Nightmares from Within

<u>DEADLY LOVE SERIES:</u>

Destructive

Addictive

About the Author

Born and raised around Houston, Jessica is a self proclaimed caffeine addict, connoisseur of inexpensive wine, and the worst driver in the state of Texas. In addition to being all of these things, she's first and foremost a wife and mom.

Growing up, she shared her mom and grandmother's love of reading. But where they leaned toward murder mysteries, Jessica was obsessed with all things romance.

When she's not nose deep in her next manuscript, you can usually find her with her kindle in hand.

Connect with Jessica now

Website: www.authorjessicaprince.com

Jessica's Princesses Reader Group

Newsletter

Instagram

Facebook

Twitter

authorjessicaprince@gmail.com